Prologue

As a history enthusiast, I spend a lot of time
researching events that pique my interest. One I
recently read about was the Copper Scroll Treasure.
The Copper Scroll was part of the extraordinary cache
of first century documents discovered in the caves at
Qumran, popularly known for the location of the Dead
Sea Scrolls.

The Copper Scroll is very different from the
other documents found in the Qumran Library. Many
believe these documents could have been cryptic
directions to a treasure. This story is about two
people's adventures as they embark on their search
for the Copper Scroll Treasure.

This book is dedicated to my family, and also to Professor Pelz, who inspired me to explore the world of History ~ with all the adventures waiting to be explored there.

Chapter One: Thief's code

I arose from my bed late in the day, and looked out the window. It was another sunny day in New York City. Gathering my stuff from the floor, I went to take a shower.

Following the smells of cooking, I went downstairs to find my wife Nadia in the kitchen making me eggs and toast. She turned to me, and smiled.

"What are you in a rush for?" she asked.

"There's a new assignment down at the docks, I responded. A train that sunk two hundred years ago was just discovered, and Nelson said we got the job of recovering anything that was inside of it."

"Well don't take all night" said Nadia.

I reached for my jacket, and ran to the car. Arriving at the dock I found Nelson already prepping the ship, and the crew.

"Kevin," Nelson shouted down the dock.
"You're on time for once, what a surprise!"

"Hey," I said. "You know me, this is something
I didn't want to miss out on." I climbed aboard, and
began to help out.

"I knew I could count on you," he responded.
"You're my best diver so I want you going down, and
searching the train. Can you do that?"

"It shouldn't be a problem," I told him.

After getting into my wet suit, and checking my
equipment, mask, and tanks, I loaded my gear into
the ship, and joined Nelson, and his crew on the deck.
We went over the scan information, and he showed
me where it looked like there were five boxes on the
submerged railcar.

"Kevin," Nelson explained, "our contract
stipulates payment on bringing all of them up."

"Understood Nelson." I responded.

When I got back from Sri Lanka, after looking for the lost Emerald of Emperor Tito's tomb, I declared that I was done circling the globe looking for lost artifacts, and treasures. I met my wife Nadia, and fell in love. She gave me the balance, and feeling of home I'd been missing in my life. Thankfully she didn't know about my dark past, and I hoped to keep it that way. Along with a colleague of mine, Bill, we found ourselves in some misadventures. Some involved alleged stolen artifacts, a few jails we spent a bit of time in, and narrowly broke out of. Then there was the harrowing moment in a prison in China, that without an inside government official...well, we might still be there. Some of the details I'd like to forget, and certainly don't want them to become common knowledge. Shaking off these thoughts, I forced myself to focus on these five boxes, and what treasures they might hold.

Nelson interrupted my thoughts, "Kevin, we're at the site of the railcar, are you ready to do this?"

"Born ready Nelson," I replied, and jumped into the frigid Hudson River. The shock of the icy-coldness consumed my body, and I froze for a few seconds. Collecting myself, I swam toward the railcar.

Nelson's radio crackled in my headset, "Do you see them?"

"Yes Nelson," I said after scanning the murky water. "It looks like there are a few crates down here."

"There better be five of them Kevin. Make sure."

I counted the crates amongst the other debris. "One, two, three...yup Nelson, five crates. I'm going to take a look inside one of them just to make sure."

"Sounds good Kevin, remember to check your oxygen, don't take too long."

I opened the first crate, Holy Smokes! "Nelson! It looks like a ton of silver bars." "Ha-ha, good stuff Kevin! This will be one of our better pulls. Let's start bringing them up," he ordered.

After bringing up the last crate, I pried open one of the crates. This one was also filled with silver bars. I started stacking them off to the side to see if the bars went all the way to the bottom of the crate. They were surprisingly heavy, and made a repetitive thunking sound as they were stacked on top of each other. As I worked my way down I noticed at the bottom of the crate, tucked into a corner of the crate, a small metal box. Excitedly, I pulled it out. After breaking open the lock I saw an old book wrapped in water-proof skins, with strange markings on it. The title was: *The Copper Scroll: Real or Fake.* Hmmm, interesting. Out of curiosity, I pocketed the book thinking this was something I'd like to explore later in private. I could only image what secrets this book might hold.

As Nelson was cataloging the contents of the crates he said, "You son of a gun. I am so proud of you!"

"Thanks Nelson," I replied. "What do you suppose this take is worth?"

"Five crates, two hundred bars in each crate, about six hundred thousand, but remember half goes to the people who paid us to do this job." I counted in my head. Thirty-thousand is still a good take. Most times it's less than a thousand. Hey, what do you say you and I go out, and have a good time tonight?"

"Thanks Nelson, but I am going home to spend some time with Nadia."

"Have it your way," Nelson laughed. "Hey Tim, are you and I going to the bars tonight?" Tim gave him a thumbs up.

After we finished cataloging the crates contents Nelson came up to me, and asked, "Are you all right?" I looked up at him, and nodded. He continued to press, "Well, you know maybe thoughts about your past are creeping into your head." I assured Nelson that life was behind me, and explained further that I hadn't seen Bill in at least ten years.

"I don't think that life is for me anymore Nelson. I am committed to the job I got now."

"Well that's good to hear Kevin. But, hey, seriously, you know how much you mean to me."

"Yeah, I know," I said leaping from the boat. Right now I got to go. I can't keep the wife waiting."

Chapter 2: Fake or Real

As I was driving home I couldn't stop thinking about the book. I pulled into the driveway, and saw Nadia through the kitchen window. She smiled, and waved at me. I opened the door, and Nadia came over, and hugged me.

"How was today?" she asked.

"Fine baby, we had a great take, thirty thousand is my take home cut." I replied.

"You can't be serious Kevin!" gasped Nadia "It's hard to digest that much money. Kevin, now you need to retire. We have the ability to do it now. We can leave New York, and go to Austria like we planned."

As we made our way into the kitchen Nadia smiled at me. "Dinner is almost done. Go clean up, you know I hate the smell of river water."

I gave her a quick peck, and went into my office. I turned to go towards the shower but remembered the book was still in my pocket. Drawing it slowly out, it seemed to be calling to me. I couldn't resist opening the cover, and turning to the first page. It read: *The Copper Scroll is part of the extraordinary cache of 1st Century documents first discovered in caves at Qumran, popularly known as the Dead Sea Scrolls. The Copper Scroll, however, is very different from the other documents in the Qumran library. In fact, it is so anomalous among the Dead Sea Scroll. The locations are written as if the reader would have an intimate knowledge of the obscure references.*

Qumran? I had never heard of it. I sat down in my chair, and looked up Qumran. With a few quick searches on my desk laptop I discovered that Qumran is an archaeological site in the West Bank managed by Israel's Qumran National Park.

I sat back in my chair, and pondered this information. OK, so we know it was found in Israel, and the book seemed to be offering clues to something. Without much hesitation I called Bill.

"Kevin to what do I owe this surprise call from you after ten years?" Understanding his surprise I filled him in. "Bill you'll never believe what I found!

It's a book about the Copper Scroll. The one they found in Qumran. This is insane Bill. I never heard of this scroll existing before. Apparently there is a treasure linked to this scroll that no one has ever found!"

There was a pause of dead air on the phone.

"Kevin," Bill finally broke in. "You and I, we both gave that life up ten years ago after we got back from Sri Lanka, barely alive. We said we would never do it again."

I understand his reservations. "Yeah Bill, I know, but this is something everyone has forgotten about. There is no way anyone is looking for this; I just uncovered this book today, buried in the Hudson River. Everyone is still on the Ark of the Covenant bandwagon search."

"Kevin," Bill said in a quieter tone, "both of us know this isn't something we should be doing. I've moved on. I own my own business. You, you got the docks, and Nadia. What do you think Nadia would do if you just up, and left for a while?"

I could hear the concern in his voice. "Well, I could tell her I have a business meeting overseas. It wouldn't be a lie considering we would in fact be overseas."

"We both know that life has come, and gone," Bill said. "We have great memories, which I will never forget but I mean, geez Kevin look at us! We're almost forty years old."

I needed Bill with me. How could I convince him this was too good to back away from? "I know it sounds crazy, but Nadia wants to retire to Austria, and I can't do that with how much I make yearly. Today I got lucky, and took home thirty thousand. Do you have any idea how rare that is? The diving year is almost up for the dock team, and I have only made fifty thousand." I paused to let this sink in. "Bill, we need to do this. This is our last one together, I promise. After this we are done forever."

"I just can't do this with you. It sounds intriguing, I'll admit, but I have a new life now."

Frantically I grasped for one last straw to try to convince him. "Look Bill, this is one of the most fabled treasures of all time. We've read of this possible existence. You can't tell me you are curious. If we find this, we are both set for life." I waited for what felt like an eternity for him to respond.

An audible sigh, "Kevin this is it, one last time," No more after this, promise?"

"Yes! I promise! No more after this. I'll delete your number from my phone, and you'll never hear from me again."

After making plans to meet at the Tel Aviv airport in two days, we said our goodbyes. As I hung up I felt as if I had made a terrible decision. I was about to go lie to Nadia and Nelson about where I am going, and why I am going there. What had I just done? Shaking me from these thoughts, I heard a shout from the kitchen.

"Kevin! Dinner has been ready for five minutes, are you coming down?"

"Yes dear, give me like four minutes," I shouted as I ran to the bathroom. I quickly finished my shower, threw on some clothes, and ran downstairs, my mind racing with excitement, and dread at what I would say to Nadia.

"Kevin, you are always doing this," Nadia said as I entered the room. 'Just one time I would like to start dinner on time."

Not a good beginning, I thought. "Sorry babe, you know how it is. Lots of paperwork after a day at the docks." We began to eat the salmon she made, and I kept quiet, not sure what I was going to say to her.

"Kevin, are you ok?"

Oh boy, I thought, well here goes. "Nadia, I don't know how to put this but I have to go to Israel for a while."

She didn't miss a beat. "Israel? But why?"

"We have a business meeting in Tel Aviv with a company that wants my help on a dive mission." Still the truth I told myself. She looked at me across the table, paused, put her fork down, and asked how long I'd be gone. I was struggling to be as evasive as I could, and still not out rightly lie to her.

"It's hard to say. I have to be at the Tel Aviv airport in two days. They are picking me up at ten in the morning. Look babe, this could be a really big take home for us, and then we can retire in Austria."

"Ok," she said. "Just be safe ok?"

Relieved, I assured her that nothing will go wrong. That was probably my worst lie that night.

We finished dinner, and spent a relaxing evening together. Later, as Nadia peacefully slept next to me, I tossed, and turned thinking about Israel, and the Copper Scroll Treasure. Was I making a mistake? Was I wrong in not telling her the truth? What equipment would I need to bring? What was I going to say to Nelson? What would our life be like after finding the treasure? These thoughts raced through my mind as the night dragged on.

I woke to my phone alarm. It was already five in the morning. Nadia, continued to snooze as I got out of bed, dressed, and headed to the car. I had a missed call from Bill so I called him back while I sat in the driveway.

"Bill, hey it's Kevin. I see I missed your call at what looks like two in the morning. What's up?"

"I don't have all the time in the world," Bill, said. "Some business things are squeezing me right now. I moved up my plans. We are leaving today instead. I found a flight from Chicago to Israel that leaves in two hours."

Was I ready for this? "Ah, today I planned to go to work, and do the prep paperwork, you know that."

"Look Kevin, I'm risking my life, and my business for this treasure that may not even exist. Find a flight, and get on it."

Can I do this now? What's holding me back? "Fine," I said. "Let me call Nelson, and see what I can do ok."

As I hung up the phone I knew I was about to lie to Nelson. That is something I never ever wanted to have to do. Taking a deep breath, I dialed his number.

"Hey Nelson, its Kevin. Look, I have to go to Austria for a few weeks. Nadia, and I are going to look at homes for retirement out there. It might be a few weeks. Are you cool with that?"

"I guess so," Nelson said after a brief pause. We're shipping the find from yesterday out today, and the slow season is starting soon anyway. We've got Greg to cover your dives while you gone. Go on, enjoy Austria."

As I hung up I knew this might not end well. I raced to the airport, and arrived at the J. F Kennedy International Airport. Making my way through the line at the ticketing desk, I finally reached the agent.

"Excuse me miss, do you have any flights from here to Tel Aviv today?"

She typed several entries into her terminal then looked up at me. "It looks like there is one seat left on the Eleven O'clock flight to Tel Aviv, but it's a first class ticket. The price is two thousand dollars."

I didn't stop to think. 'That's fine," I said.

As I walked away from the ticket desk I looked at the ticket, and thought to myself. Well, if I am about to go risk my life for one last treasure I might as well fly in style.

"All aboard flight 820 to Tel Aviv!" I looked at my ticket, and took a deep breath. I guess this is really happening. There's no going back now. I boarded the flight, and took my seat in first class. I had not flown over seas in ten years, and forgot how long the flights were. I rested in my seat, and about two hours later a flight attendant came by, and asked me, "Sir, today's lunch specials are steak and potatoes, or salmon and rice." "I'll try the salmon and rice." I looked out the window, and watched the landscape change with each passing mile.

After finishing my meal, I began looking at my laptop for more information about the Copper Scroll. A man across from me looked at me for a few seconds.

"Business or pleasure" he asked. "What brings you to Tel Aviv?"

"Oh just meeting up with an old friend."

He went on to tell me he was from Tel Aviv, and that he was a local businessman who ran a bakery.

"The names Rin, he said, "And, you are?"

"Kevin."

He shifted to get more comfortable. "Kevin huh, so is this your first time in Tel Aviv?"

"Yes sir, but I've been to a ton of different countries, and cities overseas before." "Well Kevin you must have an interesting job."

"Well I used to, but I am retired. I'm just meeting an old friend for drinks."

Rin laughed. "Drinks huh? No one flies fifteen hours for drinks. Must be some pretty good drinks! Well, whatever reason you're here, make sure to stop by my bakery. You can't miss it."

I nodded to him, and went back to my laptop. A few hours passed before Rin engaged in more conversation.

"Kevin, have you ever heard of Qumran?"

I casually closed my lap top, hoping he hadn't noticed my research. "No sir I don't think so." Had he noticed?

"A magnificent place," Rin said. "I used to be part of a team that worked that dig site twenty years ago. We found so many fossils. It was mainly human bones though. Sadly, the government had it on tight lock down, afraid someone might try to steal from the dig site."

My mind raced, could the site still be on security lockdown? I asked him if he still had access.

"Yes, well sort of," Rin said. "As an old mayor of Tel Aviv I have personal entrance access to any place in Israel. Why do you ask?"

Quickly thinking, I replied, "Well I am a history buff, and I thought it would be a cool place to see."

"Well Mr. Kevin why don't you find me at my bakery tomorrow, and I'll see what I can do."

After giving me the address I settled in for a rest. I was jolted awake when the plane was touching down. I walked out of the plane, and into the airport. There airport was a sense of wonderment to me as I made my way to baggage claim. I was waiting for my bag when I heard a shout in the distance. Several of us looked around then re-focused on the baggage carousel. From far off I hear the shouting again.

"Kevin! Kevin! It's Bill."

I looked over at Rin, and he flashed me a smile.

"I assume that's your friend," he said.

I nervously watched as Bill made his way over to me. Would Bill blow our cover, and opportunity to gain access to the site?

Bill rushed over, and stopped a few inches from me. "Kevin! Didn't you hear me calling?" Have you seen this airport? Jeez what a long flight, was I ever glad to get off the plane. Hey, who is this with you?"

"Bill, this is Rin, he is a local business owner, and former mayor. He said he could get us access to Qumran, and since we are both History buffs he agreed to do it. Rim, this is Bill, my associate I'm meeting for drinks."

Rin stepped up to shake hands. "Nice to meet you Bill. The name's Rin of Rin's Bakery in Tel Aviv. It's a pleasure to meet you. Oh, there's my bag, and it sounds like you two have some catching up to do. Meet me at my bakery in the morning, and we will set out for the Qumran dig site."

We said our goodbyes, and collected our bags. As we made our way through the airport we were inundated with the spicy smells, the noise of several different languages being spoken around us, and the crowded throngs of travelers all making their way to somewhere.

As we exited the airport Bill asked where the hotel was. "Should be two blocks down, See the building with a big clock on it? It's to the right of that." We walked up to the front hotel desk, and the man behind the desk greeted us.

"Welcome gentlemen my name is Dia. Welcome to Tel Aviv's finest hotel. Checking in I presume."

"Yes sir," we replied, "Kevin Lilly, and Bill Wright." He pulled up our reservations.

"Ok gentlemen, we have Bill in room four hundred five, and Mr. Lilly you are in the Presidential Suite."

"Really Kevin?" "What?" "The Presidential Suite."

I laughed, "Hey first time in Tel Aviv might as well go all out."

"Mr. Wright we can upgrade you to a suite for an extra hundred a night if you would like?"

Bill shrugged, "Here put it on my card, thank you Mr. Lilly."

"Alright Mr. Wright you are now relocated to Suite one. Enjoy your stay gentlemen."

We got into the elevator, and Bill started to get mad. "Kevin you didn't need to do that you know."

"Yeah I know Bill but come on, this is it, the last run we'll ever do." When the elevator stopped, I go left as Bill goes right. I glance back over my shoulder, "Bill, I confirmed for six in the morning with Rin." Bill ignored me as he entered his suite.

I looked at my phone, and noticed a missed call from Nadia. Uh-oh. I got into my suite, sat down on the bed, and called Nadia. "Hey babe it's me, yeah it's wonderful here I am going out to the dock tomorrow to dive with them for our first project." We carried on a brief conversation sharing the small details of our days. "Yup, love you too babe. I'll be home sooner than you know." Ending the call, I closed my eyes, leaned my head back, and tried to sleep, but this sense of doubt filled my mind. Could I trust Rin? Do we steal something tomorrow? As more what-if's rolled around in my head, I finally fell asleep.

Chapter 3: Qumran

I woke up to my alarm going off. Getting out of bed, I hit the shower, got dressed, and headed down to the main floor. "Mr. Lilly, so good to see you. Did you sleep well?"

Glancing up at the desk I replied, "Yes thank you Dia. Is there any breakfast options as of right now?"

"Yes sir, but why eat that pre-set food. Tell me what you would like, and the kitchen will make it for you." I told him I wasn't too picky, eggs, and toast would be fine. "Right away Mr. Lilly."

I sat down in a chair, and a few minutes Dia came over to me with a plate. "Thank you Dia." As he assured me it was his pleasure, I thought of something. "Dia, have you ever lied to someone you loved?"

He looked at me funny, and then responded, "Mr. Lilly, I have never been married but whatever you reason is I am sure it must be a good one. You seem like a good man." Dia walked away, and I laughed to myself. A good man. I've stolen more relics than some smaller museums have collected.

I look to the stairs, and watch as Bill slumps down the stairs. "You don't look too good," needling him just a bit.

"Yeah, well, you know me with my insomnia. I was up until almost one in the morning."

"Well go grab a plate, and hurry up. We can't keep Rin waiting." Bill sat down, and ate his food. As I watched him I realized how much we had both aged.

When Bill finished eating he looked at me, "You ready? What a glorious day to die." We got into a taxi, and he drove us to the front of Rin's store.

After tipping the driver we got out, and walked into the bakery, the smells immediately teasing us. Rim came out smiling with his hands extend.

"Welcome gents to the best bakery in Tel Aviv. Let me show you the around." As I walked behind Rin, feeling his pride in what he'd built, a sense of guilt came over me. We were using this guy, and I felt the weight of that guilt. "Well gents that's the bakery, any questions?"

"Nope" both Bill, and I said at the same time. Rin smiled, and waved us towards the door.

"Well you two probably want to see the Qumran Dig Site. Let's be off."

We loaded into his off-road truck, left the Tel Aviv boundaries, and made for the Qumran dig site. After driving for hours we arrived at site. I surveyed the lay of the land. It was crawling with security, and archeologists.

"Gents meet Jopi the lead archeologist of the dig site," Rin said.

Standing before us was a cheerful character with dark hair, and beady eyes. "How you do gents. Jopi is the name, archaeology is the game. So, what is your profession?"

Extending my hand I introduced myself. "I am a diver that recovers lost things in New York's river as well as being a big history buff. Bill here is a History, sorry - former History Professor at Yale."

"You two will love to see our library then." Jopi showed us around the dig site, and their tables.

I saw a skull, and said "Jopi that's from a camel right?"

"Yes Kevin, a good eye for skulls you have there." I was sort of joking but I guess he bought the bluff. "Now if you two want to see our library follow me." Jopi got into a large four wheeler, and we drove a short distance to a building. "Welcome to the Qumran Library home of many finds including the Copper Scroll."

Immediately becoming more alert, I asked, "Is this fable about the treasure of the Copper Scroll true you think Jopi?"

"Hard to say, but I like to think so, although no one has found much on it to date."

"Do you have a copy of the text from the scroll by any chance? I would love to have a copy," I said.

"Sadly, no. some of the writing is impossible to read so we don't make copies of incomplete items." Jopi seemed to like me, and Bill which is good. "So gentlemen, any questions about our library?"

"No sir." Both Bill, and I responded. By the time we finished in the library it was getting late. Jopi offered us temporary tents to spend the night, and the opportunity to join in the dig activities in the morning. But Bill reminded me that we had to be back in Tel Aviv for a meeting. "Sorry Jopi, I guess we can't stay tomorrow, but a raincheck?"

"Sure no problem you two sleep tight."

We both walked to a tent, and crawled in. We stayed up late until all were asleep, and the nigh time quiet descended upon the site. I whispered, "So Bill, you ready to steal the Copper Scroll?"

"Better now than never." We crawled out of the tent, and sneaked over to the library. I put the door cracking code device to the door, and punched in a code. The library door opened. We walked over to the Copper Scroll sitting in its case. As we lifted it up we expected alarms to sound but nothing happened. We ran outside to the four wheeler, and drove off to Tel Aviv.

"Well Bill, how do you feel about being wanted men of Israel? We have to go somewhere else, get lost in the crowds."

Bill laughed, and said, "I have an idea Kevin. Take us to the Tel Aviv docks, and we can catch a boat to Athens." We arrived at the Tel Aviv docks, and ran up to the ticket agent.

The ticketing agent looked up. "Good afternoon gentlemen, where to?"

Trying to appear calm I said, "Athens Greece."

"Ok Athens Greece, that'll be 178.08 Shekels."

We handed him the Shekels, and ran onto the dock to catch the boat. "Well Bill it's about an elven hour boat ride to Athens so get comfy." Hours went by, and soon enough we approached the coastline of Greece. The boat slowed to a halt. I suggested we find a hotel room quickly so we could study the scroll.

Watching the boat inch into the docking area, the boat was ushered into a line. "Bill, what is this?"

"What do you think Kevin, this is customs. We are coming from Tel Aviv; they are going to check our stuff."

Alarm bells went off in my head. "Bill if they see that Scroll, we are dead."

"Don't worry Kevin; these guys don't know what the Scroll is."

As we were being examined by customs I tried to play it cool. I asked the workers the best places to visit while I was here. None of them responded. I'm thinking odds are they hate their job, and don't really care who brings what in. After we got past customs, we headed to the main drag, and hailed a taxi driver.

"Where to my friends," the driver asked.

"Can you take us to downtown Athens?"

"Downtown Athens, that'll be fifty Euros."

Bill, screamed at the driver, "Fifty Euros! We just got in from Tel Aviv. How would we have Euros on us?"

The Driver grunted, not making eye contact with Bill, "No money, no taxi."

"Wait" I said. Reaching into my wallet, I handed the man seventy Euros.

He turned to me smiled, and said "I get you there fast just relax." As he went speeding through the strip, and towards downtown, Bill, and I didn't speak a single word. The cab came to a halt, "Alright you two, here we are, downtown Athens, enjoy."

We scurried out of the cab, and headed towards the right in hopes of finding a hotel. As we passed by a museum, a man opened the door to the museum, and stepped out. He shouted, "Professor Wright!?" Bill, turned towards the museum entrance confused. A young man walked down the steps towards us.

"Professor it's me, remember? I was a student of yours at Yale?"

Bill, turned on his teacher charm, "Ha-ha, I had many students while I taught at Yale. And you name was?"

"James sir, James Hill."

"Yes I remember you. You were the one who skipped the first week of class."

"Hey Mr. Wright we went over this ok, I was sick."

"James, oh James, you were one of my favorite students." "So did you ever get a PhD like you said you would?"

"Yes Mr. Wright I got a PhD in European History, and now work at the Athens History Museum."

"Good for you James." I could see Bill was trying to extract us from this reunion. "Well, it was good to see you but my friend, and I need to get going. We have to get back to our hotel. We have a business meeting. It was a pleasure running into you here. Good luck to you." Bill waved goodbye, and we walked around him, breathing a sigh of relief as we picked up our pace.

Turning the corner we saw a block of police cars lined up, and an officer stopped us. "Evening you two. We are looking for two men who made off with the Copper Scroll from the Qumran Library. Have you two been to Israel recently?"

"No sir" we both replied.

"Well if you don't mind letting us search your bags, you can be on your way." I glanced at Bill, he was calm. He didn't seem nervous at all. I tried to take a few breaths to help myself appear calm as well. The cop opened the bags, and rummaged through them for a bit. "Well you two, I found nothing in your bags that could be the Copper Scroll, so you two enjoy your time in Greece." Bill, and I picked up our bags, and calmly take a quick right, and faded away from the cops, ducking into an alley at the first opportunity.

Scanning for exits, I hissed at Bill, "We have to get back to the United States as soon as possible."

"Kevin, chill out. What do you expect we do? There are cops searching all of Europe, and Africa for two guys who stole the Copper Scroll. Need I remind you that is us?"

Trying to chill out, I asked Bill if he thought we might be able to find a small airport nearby, and possibly steal a plane to fly back to America.

"Kevin, where do you think we could possibly land? Every airport will be on alert."

Thinking of options, I suggested, should luck shine upon us, and we stumble across a small airport with a plane available for the taking, (sure, sure), we could possible land in an open field in North Dakota. Footing it to a local town we could borrow a car, and make our way back to New York. Piece of cake. Bill rolled his eyes, and swore. I took this as approval of our new plan.

We found a taxi, and got in. The driver slightly turned to glance at us as we crawled into the back seat. "Hello sirs where to?"

I responded, "Is there a nearby private airport?"

"Yes sir, the nearest one is twenty minutes away. So you folks trying to get someone to fly you? I understand. I can't stand public airlines. Just between us, I don't like to fly." He was met with silence as we gazed out the window. A couple minutes later we arrived at a locked gate. "Alright you two, we are here. Athens A-244 private airport, enjoy your flight."

We paid the driver, and got out of the taxi. Walking up to the gate a security guard waved to us. "Hello gentlemen, how can I help you today?"

"We were looking to hire a pilot to fly us to the United States; we need to get to North Dakota." I glanced around to see what planes were there.

"Let me page the pilots."

As we stood there nervously waiting for the response from the gate guard I pulled out my phone. Great, a text from Nadia. She is worried sick about me. I texted back, "Hey babe, I am on a flight back to the states. Landing in North Dakota, and then I'll be driving back to New York. I'll let you know when I get there." I then shut my phone to silence ending any further dialogue.

The gate guard looked up as he hung up his radio. "Well you two are in luck. The best pilot in all of Athens is willing to fly you. Meet him at hanger C-14."

Bill, and I shared a quick relieved smile, picked up our bags, and went to the hanger. As we got closer a rough-looking man stood there.

Slightly nodding at us, he said, "You must be the two Americans. You have cash?"

"Yes sir. I am Kevin, and this is Bill." We paid him whatever he wanted, no questions asked.

"Alright you two, let's get your bags in the storage compartment, and load you on in." Bill, and I entered the plane, and buckled in. "We'll need to make a pit stop in Spain for a gas fill up. After that, straight to North Dakota." The pilot flicked on some switches, and we seamlessly lifted off into the air, leaving behind our troubles, for now at least.

Hours passed. Eventually the pilot turned to us, and said, "Alright gents, we are twenty minutes from the North Dakota Airport. Prepare for landing." A few minutes later the plane started to violently shake from side to side. Over the intercom we hear, "Keep calm it's nothing serious." I looked out at the wing of the plane, it was burning!

"Hey pilot, the wing's on fire! I'd call that pretty serious."

His calm voice came back on, "We will be fine. Just going to put the plane down here, and we will get out fast." As soon as the plane touched down it was engulfed in flames. The sound was deafening, and smoke burned our eyes. We scrambled for our lives to leave the burning ball of flames while it was still moving. There was a screaming howl as the plane combusted, pieces of metal flying off into the night sky.

Chapter 4: Fifteen years

The sound of a phone alarm rang out through the dorm room as I got out of bed. I rubbed my eyes, and went to the bathroom to shower. Getting back to my room, I quickly got dressed, grabbed my coffee thermos, backpack, and left the dorm building. I checked my phone on the way. A new tweet from the History Channel: *"Tonight the unsolved mystery of two men who stole the Copper Scroll. Catch this special episode tonight."* I swiped my phone off, and entered the History wing located in Lincoln Hall. Entering the classroom, I sat in my usual seat directly in the middle of the classroom. I sipped my coffee while half listening to snippets of conversation drifting around me. I turned when someone called my name, "Hey Jordan did you catch the game last night?"

"Of course I saw the game," I responded. "Boston won four to three in overtime against the Jets. Wouldn't have missed that game for anything."

"Yeah, did you see who Detroit plays tonight?"

"Of course, Chicago Classic, can't wait to see it." The air in the room changed, and I sat up straight.

"Alright everyone sit down, sit down. Welcome to the first day of History two hundred and one, Early European History. I am professor Pelz. As I look across this room I see a lot of potential masters of the study of History."

I opened my notebook, dug out a pen, and leaned forward, Pelz had my full attention. "History isn't about dates; no it's about events, and their importance. You will never need to know every year, every single thing that happened. As long as you have an idea of what you're talking about, you will be fine in this class."

I shot up my hand, "Mr. Pelz, what's your take on the Copper Scroll, and the two men who stole it, and disappeared?"

"Well some think they died somewhere in America, and others think they got shot, or killed in Athens. I personally think the media obsession with this is absurd."

"Mr. Pelz!" I persisted.

"Yes?"

"Do you think the treasure is real?"

"Well the treasure of the Copper Scroll is one of life's greatest mysteries that has gone unsolved. Anyway, let's get back to today's class topic. Who in your mind was the greatest European power house in early Europe? Let's see, Jordan is it?"

"Yes Sir."

"Jordan who do you think the greatest European power was in early Europe?"

Being put on the spot, I thought for a minute. "It depends on how early, but I think the greatest empire to grace Europe was the ancient Roman Empire."

"A standard answer to say the least Jordan." So much for trying to impress the Prof the first day of class.

When class ended, I walked out into the hall. A girl walked up next to me. "Jordan is it?"

"Yeah..."

"My name's Lilly. You seem like you know a lot about History."

"Yeah well my Dad is a History Professor at the University of Michigan so he taught me a lot of what I know."

"Hey, do you think you could help me with an assignment for one of my other History classes?"

I glanced at my phone, and saw the History Channel Episode about the Copper Scroll was coming on in five hours. "Lilly, I'll tell you what. If you watch the History Channel episode on the Copper Scroll, I'll help you. I don't have a roommate so it gets boring in there."

"You got yourself a deal Jordan!" As we walked to the dorm room she asked me, "Hey your Dad isn't he the one who wrote that piece on the Lost City of Atlantis is he?"

Great, I thought, here we go again with this. "Yeah he is. He gets a lot of people stopping him to talk when he goes out anywhere."

She grabbed my arm excitedly, "I can't believe he was the one who found it! Imagine being the first one to see it since it sunk!" She looked at me more closely, "Hey! You sound depressed, what's up!"

"Well I mean having my Dad be a History professor is cool, and all but I feel like he expects me to do something on a global scale like when how he found Atlantis. He wants me to make some big find of my own. It's just a lot of pressure." Thankfully she dropped the topic, and we made it back to my dorm.

As I helped her with her homework, I started to feel this comfortable bond growing between us. She excessively thanked me for helping her. I assured her it was no big deal, which it wasn't. We finished just as the History Channel was beginning its episode on the Copper Scroll. Perfect timing. "Evening everyone, I am Doctor Grant Lewis, and tonight on the History Channel, we will explore the Copper Scroll gone missing, and the theory of the two men who stole it to find the treasure linked to the Scroll."

We watched the show, and as it got to the last few minutes, something they said made me think.

"Well folks, as of today we can confirm that the plane the two men flew in to North Dakota did in fact blow up. Whether the men inside survived is unconfirmed. There were no remains at the site. Their graves are in North Dakota, and thousands of people have visited them, to marvel or condemn the two men who caused this global mystery. Thanks for watching tonight's episode. I'm Grant Lewis, and remember to go out, and seek your own History." As the episode ended I remained quiet, and awe struck.

Lilly broke the silence, "Well Jordan, I should get back to my room, and get to bed. Hey, you alright?"

I started to think of possibilities. "Lilly, what if they left a clue in North Dakota for people to find the treasure."

Lilly laughed, "Jordan we are just college students. We wouldn't even know where to begin."

As we discussed this in more detail the excitement began to envelope Lilly. Was there a chance there was a clue out there that no one had discovered yet? Maybe this was my find. "Lilly, let me call my Dad. He might have an idea about this."

Lilly started to gather her books, "I guess, besides I could use a weekend trip somewhere. Thanks again for helping me with my homework. I had fun today. "

As soon as Lilly left my room, I called my Dad." Hey Dad, it's Jordan! I'm doing great. The first day of class was good." We chatted more about school, and classes, how much homework I had, and then I veered the conversation in a different direction. "Dad, do you know anything about the Copper Scroll? I just saw the History Channel episode on it, and kind of wondered what you knew about this." He surprised me by stating the two men weren't buried in North Dakota, but South Dakota. He went onto discuss more details not covered on the episode. I think he sensed my excitement, and reminded me I was a student, my focus should be on my school work. I quickly assured I wouldn't do anything crazy, told him I loved him, and hung up. I texted Lilly right away, telling her my Dad told me some stuff about the Copper Scroll, and I needed to talk to you about it tomorrow.

I was eating lunch in the cafeteria the next day when Lilly came up to me, and sat down, asking what I found out about the Scroll. "Lilly, this isn't exactly the best place to talk about that. Meet me in the library tonight at midnight."

She looked at me unsure, "But Jordan, the library closes at ten?" I smiled, and winked at her, "It's alright. I got a man on the inside. Meet me outside at midnight."

I went to my remaining classes, got to the library, and stood outside waiting for Lilly. Just as I started to give up hope that she wasn't coming, she snuck up behind me, and, poked me in the back. I spun around, "Lilly, please don't do that!"

"Sorry but this is what you get for making me come to the library this late at night, when I could be sleeping."

I started walking towards the library door, "It's for a good reason I swear Lilly!" I went to the library door, and Lilly, followed.

The door opened, a man greeted us, "How long you need Jordan?"

"Give me two hours Kyle, and hey thanks so much for this."

"No problem Jordan, I owed you anyways."

I walked to a corner of the library, and sat down. Lilly sat down next to me. "So Jordan what is so important?"

"Lilly I talked to my Dad last night he told me something about the Copper Scroll."

"Jordan we are college students. We can't just dump college to chase after a treasure that might not even be real."

"Lilly, we have to do this now or we may never get this chance again. We have all the time in the world for college but this is happening now. I called my Dad, Lilly. He said it's in South Dakota. The scroll is for sure there!"

She looked at me, "How is that possible? The two guys who stole it died in North Dakota?"

I moved closer to her, and lowered my voice. "It's complex. As it turns out, none of them died. They got out of the plane before the plane blew up. They traveled south in hopes of finding a place to stay. Making it to South Dakota, they died after getting shot by the FBI. Turns out once word got to America that two Americans had stolen the Copper Scroll, the FBI locked onto all planes as they flew into United States air space."

Lilly asked, "The FBI shot the two men? So where does that come into play with the scroll Jordan?"

I started to pace a bit with excitement, "The FBI only had orders to shoot them. They left the bodies in a morgue to be searched the next day, but someone stole the body of the man with the scroll. They buried him in South Dakota with only one clue ever known on to how to find his grave."

"Well what's the clue?"

I glanced at my phone where I had made the clue notation, "To find the scroll you must repent your soul."

Lilly jumped up, "So he is at a church?"

I took a deep breath, "Well, see, that's where it gets tricky because I cross- referenced all the churches in South Dakota, and none of them have records of receiving a body for burial on the day he was claimed to be buried. My Dad said there is an old rundown church nearby that had old records of a burial on that day in 1953. It's since been shut down, and deserted. I'm thinking, no one is looking into abandoned churches."

"So why is he in this church though?"

"Well the rumor is the man who stole his body also has a vested interest in the scroll. He buried him in a crypt in this old church thinking no one else would look there, and then published the clue in the newspaper."

Lilly started to pace along with me, "What you are suggesting we do is fly to South Dakota, and look inside a rundown church for a dead person's body. After that, we find a scroll that will lead us to a treasure that might, or might not, be real?"

I smiled at her, "Yes, that's pretty much it."

"If my parents find out I left campus for more than a week they would call the cops to look for me. This is insane. I just met you!" She took a deep breath, and exhaled. "If I do this, is there a chance of me dying?"

I moved over to be near her, "Lilly I have no idea what is going to happen. All I know is there is treasure linked to this scroll, and I want to find it. Plus, I'll be able to gloat to my Dad. I got two tickets to

South Dakota leaving tomorrow evening. Are you in or out? It's your choice."

"This is crazy. What do we do if there is no scroll there?"

"Well," I smiled. "Then we come back to the campus, go back to our classes, and say we had a crazy adventure treasure hunting over the weekend."

"Ok, I'm in, but I'll give you two days to find the scroll. If we don't have it by then, I am coming back to campus. Do I make myself clear?"

I grabbed her in a quick hug, "Crystal clear. Trust me, it will all go smoothly." As we left the library, and walked to my dorm, I started to have feelings of doubt. Could I actually find this scroll? Adding to that, now I didn't want to let Lilly, down.

The next day arose, I cleaned up, and meet Lilly for breakfast. "Hey Mr. Hot Shot Treasure Hunter," she chuckled, as I sat down with my food. "Any doubts fill your head last night that maybe this is all just one big hoax, and we are going to make fools out of ourselves?"

"Nope!" I continued to enjoy waffles knowing this could be the last time I eat a hot meal for a while. As I ate my breakfast I listened to Lilly tell me about how her father is a surgeon at a hospital. She shared stories of different surgeries he has performed. It was nice to learn more about her. While we finished breakfast we talked about what we'd need to take with us, and the initial plans of getting there. After breakfast we went to our dorms, and packed. Meeting at an arranged spot on campus, we waited for the taxi I'd called for. When it arrived, we grabbed our backpacks, and jumped in. I looked back at the school campus wondering when I'd be back, and how changed I might be from this journey. We squeezed into the taxi, and I told the driver to take us to the airport.

"You two know it's Wednesday, right?"

I responded, "Yeah we know."

"So, no classes the rest of this week?"

"No sir," I said. I got a look from Lilly as she was stifling a laugh, knowing that I was lying to a taxi driver about missing classes.

"So, you two dating?"

"Oh goodness no," Lilly said. I looked at her, and gave her a dead eyed look as she giggled.

"So, where you two off to?"

I looked at Lilly confused, as if I should keep lying to this taxi driver, and decided its best I don't tell him the truth. "Arizona." He just nodded, and kept driving.

We got to the airport entrance, and I as I paid him Lilly stood outside the door to the airport, frozen in place. I walked up to her. "Lilly, are you alright?"

"Jordan this is a little silly don't you think?"

"Oh geez, give it a break. You already committed, and I can't believe now of all times you are having second thoughts! Look, I promise nothing is going to happen to you. Please trust me." We went through security, and made our way to the gate.

While we were sitting down I got a text from my Dad saying, "Hey Jordan I am coming to Boston this weekend, want to meet up?" I already lied to the taxi driver, now I have to lie to my Dad. Great. I texted him back, and said, "Sorry Dad, I can't meet up this weekend. I am going to New York with friends. Maybe next time" I then turned my phone off. I glanced over at Lilly. She was focused on her phone, and didn't seem to notice my texts.

The lady at the airport desk called out boarding group B. We walked up, and handed her our tickets. After getting on the plane, and finding our seats, we sat down next to this man who was in the window seat. He smiled at me, and I nodded. "So how about them Celtics," he asked me.

"Yeah they are pretty good, but I am a Detroit fan." He then proceeded to ask me about the draft, and we ended up talking about basketball for most of the flight. Lilly dozed with her head on my shoulder. Before I knew it we were landing in South Dakota.

Chapter 5: South Dakota

As Lilly and I walked out into the airport we noticed how small the airport was. We made our way to the car rental counter. The agent waved us over, "Hello you two! Welcome to Fox Car Rentals. What kind of car do you need?"

I pulled out my wallet, and said, "How about a jeep sir, we plan to do some off road driving." He handed us the keys to the jeep, and I took care of the paperwork. We made our way to the car. "You know Jordan, if we get back to campus in time we can watch the game." The game was the last thing on my mind. I was dedicated to finding this treasure, and didn't care about anything else. I didn't bother to respond.

We drove off into a South Dakota sunset, heading towards the Church of Ever Soul. I was surprised to see other cars there as we approached the church. Pulling up, I could make out a man in a uniform holding a gun. What the heck?! I quickly turned left out of sight, and turned the car off. "Jordan what are we doing?"

I put my hand over her mouth to quiet her, and not alert the gunman. I slowly let my hand go. "Lilly, those guys are from the International Affairs. This is a secret branch of United States intelligence that deals with things they want to keep quiet from the public."

Her eyes widened in fear. "So what are they doing here?"

"Isn't clear? They were assigned here by the government to find the treasure." I survey the land, and spot about ten people in uniforms with guns. I felt like the place we had parked was hidden from their view, so we were safe from them seeing us. "OK, here's the plan. With the sun setting, my guess is they'll be leaving here within a couple of hours. I say we sit tight, wait for them to go, and then we can have a look around."

Lilly nods her head at me in agreement. We sit in silence as the time passes by slowly. The sun fades into the background, and I hear engines start up. We watch as seven trucks leave the church ground, and head north into a town. I hop out of the car, and motion for Lilly to follow me. We turn a corner to find a guard keeping his post near the front of the church. I whisper, "Damn, they kept a guard here to make sure no one sneaks in. Wait, I have an idea!" I pull out my phone, and open an app a friend showed me once. I create a false radio broadcast which searches local broadband connections, and goes to the guard's walkie-talkie. "Attention, any personnel at the Church of Ever Soul. We are having a meeting at the cafe on Hummingbird Avenue. Leave now." The guard heads towards what looks like the last truck in the lot, gets in, and leaves the area.

I turn to Lilly, "That bought us about twenty minutes of time. We have to hurry up."

"How did you do that?"

I smile at her, "A good magician never tells his secrets." I pull up a map of the church on my phone. "Alright, so I don't think they made it to the catacombs yet because no one knows where that is. There is no version of a map telling where it's at, but I know." I sprint into the church, and as I enter, a sense of wonder overcomes me. I blink my eyes a few times. "We need to make this fast so don't get distracted . We need to go to the bookcase, and remove the top left book on the highest self. This will reveal the catacombs." We race towards the bookshelf, pull the book out, and the bookshelf rotates. A set of stairs heading down into the dark comes into view. I turn on my flashlight, and sprint down the steps with Lilly following close behind.

As we reach the floor of the catacombs I look around, "Ok, we need to find the tomb of Bill Wright. Spread out." The tombs are covered in dust. We spend precious minutes reading each one. I walk up to one in the back, and read, *"Bill Wright, the most wanted man in history."* "Lilly this is it! This is his tomb!" Lilly helps me move remove the top of the tomb, and we peer into a dried up skeleton residing in the coffin. "Where is it!" I yell with frustration.

"Well Jordan, it's not here. I guess no one knows where it's at." I scan the room, and see something above the tomb.

"Lilly, look! It's Greek writing. We focus in the dim light, and read, *"You have come this far in search of the scroll. At the far end of the catacombs is a door to a room that houses the Copper Scroll."* It dawns on me. "This all makes sense now! The last place they were in was Greece before coming here. He asked the pilot how to write this in Greek!"

Lilly turned to me, "Wait, I thought they all died in the plane crash?"

"No, Bill survived but couldn't continue the journey without Kevin, so he wrote this message in Greek. When he died he was buried in this exact spot above the message." I look at my watch, and panic. "We need to get to the door grab, the scroll, and leave this area in ten minutes." We sprint as fast we can to the door, fling it open, and sitting on a pedestal is the Copper Scroll. I ignore the fact I am in the presence of a true piece of history, and throw it into my backpack. Turing quickly, I grab Lilly's hand, and pull her out of the Church. We race back to the Jeep. I rev the engine, and speed out of the church area, driving off into the dark night.

Chapter 6: A new day

I wake to Lilly pacing the room. Half sitting up I ask her, "What's wrong?"

She whirls around, and screams in my face, "Jordan we stole the damn thing, and we have no plan!"

I stare at her, and take a minute to wake up. I sit Lilly down in a chair, "Lilly, I am going to call my Dad. He will know what to do."

She snorted, "Great idea, but hey, you might as well let the NSA know we have the damn Copper Scroll. The FBI, CIA, and swat teams will swarm us in five seconds." She put her head down in desperation. "No, absolutely not Jordan. We are not getting him involved at all. He will have you turn the scroll in right away, and we will never find the treasure. I've been thinking, we find the treasure, then we donate the treasure, and the scroll to a museum."

I look at her dumbfounded. "You want to just hand over the treasure to a museum! Are you out of your mind? They will be forced to turn it over to the government as soon as we hand it to a museum." We argue for an hour, and finally I break. "Let's give up, this is all moot. The government wants the treasure, we want the treasure, and museums want it. It's too much of a coveted relic of importance." Lilly slumps in her chair, and begins to cry, I scrub my hands into my face, go to the sink, and splash my face with water. I return to Lilly wiping her tears off her face. I kneel down in front of her. "Here's the plan. We find the treasure, obviously. We then return the Copper Scroll, and the treasure to the Qumran library. The place Kevin and Bill stole it from. It belongs there." Lilly blinks, and nods in agreement.

I stand up, and look at my phone, four hundred text messages, and one hundred fifty-two missed calls. Hmmm, seems a little excessive for a Thursday. After studying the Scroll I turn to Lilly. "I know where to start off with this. There are five relics spread throughout the world. When you have all five you bring them to someone called The Keeper."

"Who is this Keeper?"

"The Keeper is a family succession order of a society that awaits the true holder of the relics with the treasure lost long ago."

"Wait, the treasure has been around this whole time!"

"Yeah," I say. "It appears that way from what the scroll says. It says there are five relics. When you find them, you are to bring them to a place called Niue, it's a small island. The Keeper resides on top of a cliff, on the island, in a small house."

"You really want to do this? We could get hurt, we could die, we could..."

"Lilly, we will be fine. I promise I will not let anything happen to you. We can do this." I look into Lilly's eyes, and see she is eager to get started. Probably eager to get this over with.

"So, where are these five relics located? We should get started on this right now." We go over the relic locations noted on the Scroll. I stand to stretch, and sum it up

"Ok, the first one says Scotland, another one says Egypt, and the three others are Japan, Australia, and the last one is in North America."

"Where does it say it's located in North America?"

"Wyoming, it appears it's located at Yellowstone National Park." We look at each other, our work is cut out for us. "Well Lilly, what do you say we get some food, and hit the road to Wyoming."

"Jordan, you realize this journey could be dangerous. We need proper gear, grappling hooks...maybe even a gun."

"Stop! You are overthinking this," I try to reassure her.

"All I am saying is we should be prepared for anything."

I sigh, "Ok, we will buy a gun, grappling hook, two backpacks, a few waters, and some food to bring with us. But we are only using the gun for a dire situation of danger, understood."

"Yes I understand."

"Good, now let me get a fresh change of clothes, and we will go eat breakfast."

I leave my room, and I look at my phone again. Damn, Dad will not stop texting me. I wonder what it's about. I open my texts with my Dad, and I see a big long message from him. *"Jordan you have not responded to me in two days. Professor Rivers emailed me saying you missed his class, and I know it's not like you to miss classes Jordan. Please respond to me, so I know everything is ok with you. It's not like you if you went off in search of the Scroll because if you did, you and I are going to have a long talk about this."* I close my phone, and sigh as I look at Lilly, who is scrolling through some social media app. She looks at me with worrisome eyes, and goes back to her phone.

We get to the breakfast area of the hotel, and I grab a plate, and sit down with Lilly, "Hey, phones down when we eat Lilly."

She glares at me with - you are not my Dad - eyes, and starts to pick at her eggs. "Jordan, I need to ask you something, and you have to answer me, ok?"

"Sure, what is it?"

"Why are you at a public college? Your Dad's rated the number one professor in all of the world, has written thirty books, won a Nobel Peace Prize, you guys have five homes, fifteen cars, like you could go to any college. What made you pick ours? Like why not a private school or Yale, Brown, or some Ivy league school. What drew you to Boston of all places, for college?"

I stare in silence, and stir my coffee for a bit. So that's what she's been searching on her phone. Fair enough. I respond, "Well, I loved the Boston area when I went to a Detroit vs Boston game. I loved the city feel, and the people were great, and also because my Dad went there. I thought if I could capture his experience of college, one day I could be a great historian like him." Lilly giggled, happy she had forced the answer out of me. "Imagine being the son of the world's most famous historian, and professor. Talk about pressure! Try having your bedtime story be about the Roman Empire when you're eight."

We continue on in silence for a bit then Lilly asks, "Why did you ask me to do this with you?"

"Ask you to do what?"

"You know what I mean. Why did you bring me into this with you?"

I paused, and took a sip of my coffee. "I brought you along because I trust you."

She blinked. "You trust me? Jordan, we have only known each other for one day."

"Hey, I am pretty sure you said yes. Also, we met before."

"What do you mean?" I could see she was trying to remember ever meeting me before.

I panicked thinking I shouldn't have said that. "Do you remember your job during high school?"

"Yeah, I worked at a smoothie bar in New York."

"Exactly, we met before at the smoothie bar a year ago."

Lilly's eyes narrowed, "What do you mean?"

"My Dad brought me with him to New York for the opening of his new museum, and I we walked into your smoothie bar. You gave me this look, and kept your eyes on me while another clerk took our order".

"Wait, that was you?"

"Lilly I trusted you because when I watched you work, you were kind, and always had a smile on your face. I felt like I knew you already.

Lilly looked in wonderment at me, "Jordan, I am speechless. Why didn't you tell me this sooner?"

"I felt now was a good time, as we are about to embark on an impossible journey to find these five relics." Lilly looked down into her coffee with a closed off look on her face. Was she uncomfortable with what I had just told her? She starts to open her mouth to say something, but decides not to. Breaking the silence, I stand, "Lilly we should hit the road to Wyoming." I smile at her, and she flashes a small smile back.

As I climb into the car, Lilly looks down the road as if she is wondering if she should go back to Boston. She looks at me, and then steps into the car. "So I take it you trust me?"

She slugs me on the shoulder, and smiles at me, "Well Jordan, if we are going to defy death we might as well do it together." I smile at her, and we drive off towards Wyoming.

As we drive we talk about sports, history, art, and other topics. It was nice to spend this time getting to know her better. Suddenly Lilly stops talking, and looks at me. "Do you plan on going back to college in Boston after this?"

"Why do you ask?"

"Well college wouldn't be the same without you."

I try to avoid the question for a while, and focus on the road, but she asks me again as if I didn't hear it the first time. "If we find these five relics, get the treasure, and bring the treasure, and the scroll back to Qumran, I will not be going back to college in Boston." Lilly looks at me, and a tear drops down her face. She turns away from me. After a few seconds of quietly crying she summons the strength to ask me why. "Lilly if we do this, I won't need to finish college. I'll be incredibly busy cataloging everything, setting up my foundation, getting funding, and grants for my next historical adventure."

I drive the next few miles with her in silence while she thumbs through her phone. She finally asks me something I didn't expect. "Jordan, do you have feelings for me?

"What! Lilly, what the heck! That is so random!"

"Answer the question Jordan!"

I roll my eyes. She looks at me while sitting on the edge of her seat. "Lilly I don't have time for this stuff. We are on a mission, remember." Lilly sighs, and sits back in her seat, and eventually pulls out her phone. "Lilly you haven't told anyone what we are doing, have you?"

"No, of course not, that's the dumbest thing we could do. We are basically fugitives of the law." I glance up ahead, and see a sign that says *Welcome to Wyoming,* and decide after a long day of driving it's best for us to get some rest. I pull into a hotel parking lot, we get out of the car, and head inside. The desk clerk cheerfully welcomed us, "Welcome to Buffalo Creek Hotel, I am Jason."

"Hi Jason," I reply, "I need a room for the night."

"All we have available is the honeymoon suite. We are currently full as it's the height of Yellowstone Park's tourist season."

I glance at Lilly. "What's the cost of the room Jason? "

"Five hundred."

I feel as if my heart just stopped. I had to do whatever it took to find these relics, and if that meant spending five hundred on a hotel room, then I had to suck that up. I look at a drowsy Lilly as she yawns. "We'll take it," and I hand Jason my card.

He runs it through, and cheerfully says, "Alright you two, floor five, at the far left. Enjoy your stay."

We climb into the elevator, arriving on the fifth floor and head to the left. Lilly opens the door to the honeymoon suite, and drops here stuff on the floor. She is stunned by the size of the room. I walk past her, and jump onto the bed, flipping on the television. Lilly looks at me. "Jordan look at the size of this room!" Lilly grew up in a small apartment in New York City, so to her this is a shock. I had to admit, it was a really nice room, but I was trying to play it cool. I shoot her a grin. Lilly glanced around the room. "Jordan, there is only one bed."

"Yes that's how it is in a honeymoon suite. We are just two people on a mission to find the treasure of the Copper Scroll. It's not like we just got married." Lilly giggles, and nods at me. She climbs into the bed, exhausted, and rolls onto her side. I glance at my phone while she starts to drop off to sleep. I put my phone down, and roll over onto my side. Suddenly I feel something on my hand. Looking down I see Lilly is holding my hand. I stay still. Unsure, I squeeze her hand. We stay that way until we both fall asleep.

Morning arrives, and I look over at Lilly still snoozing. I get up, hit the shower, and get dressed. As I come out of the bathroom I see Lilly half awake. "Good morning sleepy head, it's time to get to business. No more hotel visits. The next time we get to sleep will be on a plane to Scotland. From now on we are not taking any rest, the relics are waiting for us." Lilly nods, and I grab my stuff. We head out to the car, and climb in. I drive off into the morning sunrise towards Yellowstone Park, and pull up to the park entrance.

We are greeted by the Park Ranger, "Good morning. Welcome to Yellowstone National Park. I am ranger Rick. Go ahead, and pull into parking lot C." Once we park the car we get out, and I look at Lilly. We nod at each other silently confirming we know it's time to get to work at finding the first relic.

Chapter 7: Yellowstone Heirloom

I pull out a map to Yellowstone Park, and we pour over it together. Tracing an area on the map I nod my head, and say, "Alright, we are at parking lot C. The location of the relic is in this cave, about seven miles to the east of here."

"Jordan, I don't think we are allowed into those parts of the park."

I sigh, "Look, we are going to have to break a few laws in order to find these relics, so we might as well start with law number one. The park closes in eight hours. We need to find the relic, leaving us enough time to get back to the car, and leave before the park closes."

"Alright, but if we're caught I'm giving them a fake name!" Grab what we'll need, and let's get going."

I look both ways, and start walking towards a mountain. Seeing a river leading towards the area we need to get to, I look around for possible options of getting there. Suddenly I hear a man announcing, "Rafts for the day, ten dollars." Talk about being in the right place at the right time. I approach the man, pay him, and fill out the paperwork. We get into the raft, toss our stuff in, and start to paddle towards the cave where we think the relic is.

We pass other rafters as we head out. We consult the map, checking to make sure we're heading in the right direction. Finding a rhythm with each other's paddling we skim through the water at a smooth pace. Suddenly we come upon a deep drop off. Where was this on the map?! We brace for impact. Understandably, Lilly is freaking out. We go over the top, and plunge into the water at the bottom of the drop off. The raft pops back up, and I climb back in to the raft, frantically looking around for Lilly, shouting out her name. Within a few seconds I see her struggling to get out of the water on the rocky shore. I dive out of the raft, and swim the few yards towards her. Grabbing her arms, I pull her out of the water, and onto the rocks nearby. She is struggling to breathe so I immediately begin mouth to mouth resuscitation. A few seconds later she spits water up into my face, and opens her eyes. Taking a deep breath she smiles at me. I look down at her, and say, "I told you I wouldn't let anything bad happen to you, I gave you my word." Lilly takes a few minutes to collect herself, and I look around to assess our situation. We lost the raft but we still have our backpacks, and the map.

She finally stands up, and looks out over the river. "Jordan, where did our raft go?"

"Well it was either save the raft or save you, and of course I chose to save you." We discuss our options, and determine we are a few miles away from the cave. Our only option is to go on foot. As we travel along what barely resembles paths, Lilly attempts to occupy me with playing eye-spy. As there's not a lot of variety along our journey, she soon gets bored with the game, and begins to tell me about her father. We pass the distance sharing stories of growing up. Rounding a bend, we approach what looks like a farm. A man is standing outside with a horse. We walk up to the farmer; he tips his hat at us, "Hello there folks, the name's Dave. You two are lost from what I can tell."

Surprised, Lilly asks, "How do you know that?"

"Well, I don't see a whole lot of folks out in these parts, and from what I can see, you two are in need of transportation. We nod in assent. "I'll tell you what, you two can borrow this horse of mine. When you get to where you need to be just brush her tail, and she will come running back home."

Overwhelmed with gratitude, I ask Dave, "What do I owe you for this?"

He replied, "There is no need for payment young one." As the horse is already saddled he runs through the basics, and confirms that I've ridden before. I mount the horse, and reach a hand down to Lilly. She grabs a hold, and with Dave's help, we lift her onto the horse behind me. Dave waves goodbye, and walks away.

Lilly giggles. "Jordan do you even know how to ride a horse?"

"You know us silver spoon guys, I've spent a few summers riding on the ranch." She wraps her arms around my waist to hold on, and with that I turn the horse in the direction we want to go, nudging her into a run. The trail we are on is much more open. I look back to see Lilly enjoying the ride, and smiling harder than I have seen before. Making up much of the lost time, we pull up to the cave entrance sooner than I thought possible. I jump off the horse, and help Lilly down. Brushing the horse's tail, it turns, and heads off towards the farm.

I glance over at Lilly, and notice she has a blank look in her eyes. Waving my hand in front of her, trying to get her attention, I ask, "What's wrong?"

She points to the cave, "Do you realize what cave this is?"

"No, it's just a cave, and I just got to it."

She's speaking louder now, and stuttering over her words, "Jordan this is the Cave of Ice."

I blink twice, and look at Lilly confused. "So, what is this Cave of Ice?"

She looks at me amazed that I don't know this. "Legend says The Cave of Ice is a cave that engulfs half of those who enter it. History suggests it may be the most dangerous cave in all of North America. Apparently there are a series of puzzles, and traps you need to figure out once you're inside. One wrong step, and POOF, you're gone."

Seriously? How have I never heard of this? Lilly is looking at me with terrified eyes. I'm not feeling so great myself. I swallow the large lump in the back of my throat, take a deep breath, and give her a reassuring smile. Alright, I tell myself. I need to man this up. There's no turning back, and I need to make sure we both get through this. I made a promise I'd keep her safe. I'm not leaving that cave until we get what we came for.

We step inside the cave, and instantly the temperature drops several degrees. Lilly digs through her water-logged backpack for her gloves, and hat. I throw my coat on. We both pull out our flashlights, thankful they still work. Nodding at each other we venture deeper into the cave. We walk for some time, and come to a door. Etched into the door is a vase, and next to the door is a pedestal. My mind races.

"Jordan, what do you think the vase is all about?"

"Well if my memory serves me correct, there was an early tribe of settlers in Colorado called the Frost Wolves. They were a sacred tribe that were known for creating sculptures out of ice. My best guess is they had a part in making this cave."

She asks me, "Are we supposed to find this vase? Where? Are there any clues where to look?" To the left of the door is a pond of water. I know, with temperatures this cold, I could possibly freeze to death in a relatively short period of time.

"Lilly, I am about to do something really dumb, and I need you to trust me. If I don't come up within thirty seconds, pull me out."

"What!?"

Before Lilly can say another word I tear my coat off, and sprint towards the pond plunging myself into the water. Instant painful icy water envelopes me as I fight for every breath. I reach my hands down to the bottom, and flounder around trying to find anything buried in the muck. Frantically I move across the pond floor knowing I'm running out of time. At last my hand brushes against something firm with a rim. I grab onto it, and push myself to the surface. I crawl out, soaked, shivering, and holding the vase. Lilly watches me with her mouth open in shock. I grab my coat from the ground and hurriedly put it on, pumping my hands up, and down my arms to warm myself up. "Jordan have you lost your damn mind! You could have died."

Still shivering, I say, "Lilly, there is nothing I won't do to find this treasure." Smiling with success, I strut up to the pedestal, and place the vase on it. The pedestal sinks into the ground, and the pedestal floats back up with a key on its surface. "Lilly, will you please do the honors?" Lilly grabs the key, turns to the door, and inserts it into the keyhole. The door swings open. Stepping forward, we glance at each other in amazement at what just happened.

Entering the next room we both start looking for the next puzzle or clue. I come up to a statue, and freeze in place. "Lilly come take a look at this!" We stare at it in shock. It's a statue of a wolf carved out of ice but this was no average wolf. It was half wolf-half man.

Reaching out to touch it Lilly asks, "Jordan what is this statue?"

"Well, I think the legend of the Frost Wolf tribe is that they believe a half wolf-half woman gave birth to all life. Those who have a mark of the Frost wolf are immortal, or so says the myth."

"Have they ever found a person with the marking of the Frost Wolf on them?"

"Of course not. These are just stories the tribe would tell the youth to get them to bed. Sure, the tribe existed, but these are fables the tribe would hold close to them. It's unlikely there is a person with this supposed Frost Wolf marking on them."

Just as Lilly touches the statue the ground begins to shake. "What's going on?"

I glance around us, "I have no idea. Grab ahold of the statue!" We cling for life on the statue, and suddenly an explosion blows open an area of the wall.

I make out a figure walking towards us, and I can see that it seems to be human.

Wide eyed with fright Lilly asks, "Are we alright?"

"Ah, sure, for now we might be." The man emerges from the cloud of smoke, and his full figure comes into view. Standing in front of us is a figure with the top half of her body human, and the bottom half wolf.

"Greetings brave adventurers .I am Gwen the Grey, and you have are the first humans to figure out the first puzzle of our great lair." We stand there mouths gaping as we stare at what seems is impossible.

I scream out, "You're a Frost Wolf!"

"Indeed I am young lad. We Frost Wolves are immortal, and have been awaiting the day for the chosen one to seek us out."

"Well Gwen the Grey, I must admit we are here for the relic of Ice that we need as one of five to collect for the treasure of the Copper Scroll."

"What is your name lad?"

"Jordan."

"And, you young lady?"

"Lilly."

"Lilly, and Jordan, I now declare you honorary members of the Frost Wolf Tribe!"

"Gwen, thank you for that honor, but like I said, we came for the relic of ice. I mean this is amazing, and all, but I must fulfill my own legacy."

"Jordan don't you get it?"

"No Gwen I don't understand.

She replied, "The relic is my people! We are a myth. No one thought we existed. When we lived outside this cave a man came to us, and asked us to design a relic made of ice that would not melt, so we did."

"Gwen the Grey I am honored to be in your presence, and trust me when this is over I want to come, and ask many questions that I now have, but I am afraid this Copper Scroll is my calling."

"I understand Jordan, follow me, and I will get you the relic." As we follow Gwen I couldn't keep my eyes off her wolf like legs, and feet. I was in awe at this, and thought to myself, Ha! Take that Dad! I found a mythical tribe, and you haven't. We enter a room, and standing in a circle is all half wolf - half humans, some are eight feet tall. "Ice Wolves these are the chosen ones. I present to you Jordan, and Lilly." The Ice Wolves clap, and then they begin to sign a song, and as they sing an ice platform rises us all into the air. We stand there in shock, and then the platform stops. An Ice Wolf steps forward, and presses a button on the platform, and all the other Ice Wolves take a step forward, and light up a button. A pedestal rises from the ground, and stops in its place.

The leader of the Ice Wolves steps forward," Jordan I am Huko the Holy. As leader of the Ice Wolves I present to you the relic of ice, guard it with your life, and let no one but the Keeper of the Treasure hold it, understood?"

"Yes Huko the Holy, I understand," I solemnly respond.

He grabs the relic wrapped in cloth, and approaches me. He kneels down in front of me. "Jordan, I present to you the relic of ice." Huko unwraps the cloth, and inside is an ice carved book glimmering in the light. He holds it out to me, and I reverently take the relic of ice. "Jordan, this book contains the truth of the Ice Wolf Tribe. Please take good care of it. Only is this to ever touch the hands of the Treasure Keeper, do you understand me?"

"Yes Huko the Holy, I understand."

We begin to descend back to the main floor of the room, and Lilly is frozen in place, stunned by what she just saw. "Jordan before you go I must have a word with you!"

I turn to face Huko, and he takes out some sort of pouch, and motions me closer. "Jordan do you know what this bag is by any chance?"

"No Huko the Holy, I have no idea."

"Jordan this is the bag of ice. It's a holy symbol in our tribe. Inside is a frosted type ash that when touched will bound you to the Ice Wolf Tribe forever." I glance at Lilly who is still frozen in place out of shock.

"Lilly, please come here." Lilly approaches me with a blank face. "Hold out your arm please." Lilly puts her hand out and I sprinkle the ash on her arm. The ash forms into the shape of the Frost Wolf Tribe symbol.

"Jordan, please allow me," I hand Huko the Holy, the bag, and I lend him my arm.

"No Jordan, not your arm. Please show me your heart." I take my coat, and shirt off, and Huko the Holy draws a heart on my chest. The symbol of the Frost Wolf Tribe forms, but a different symbol from that of Lilly's.

"Huko, what is this symbol?"

"Jordan, I now bless you as a Prince, and future King of the Frost Wolf Tribe."

I stand in front of Huko stunned by what he just said to me. "Huko I don't understand, what do you mean?"

"Jordan, eventually us tribe folk ascend to a place called the Tree of Life where we spend our afterlife as guardians of nature. When my body ascends to the Tree of Life you will be in charge of leading the tribe." The information is too much to handle, and I collapse to my knees, and pass out.

I feel a splash of water on my face followed by more. "You can stop that now," I sputter. Lifting my head up, I look around the room, and see Lilly talking to some of the tribe's women, and eating some kind of food. Standing over me is Huko.

"Good morning sleepy head, you passed out on me."

"What do you expect Huko, it's a lot to take in." I did feel a little ashamed that I passed out. "Huko, I need to get back to the park. Lilly and I need to leave for a plane to Egypt."

"Do not worry young Prince, we took care of that for you." "What do you mean Huko?

"Well you aren't in Yellowstone Park anymore. You are near it though. We brought you to your car, and Lilly drove us to an old camp ground we had way back in the days."

"I need to book a flight from Colorado to Egypt though, and there was limited seating when I looked!"

"I got you covered Jordan. I got you two tickets via your phone."

"You went through my phone!"

"No, Lilly did. She also paid for it."

"Lilly is this true?" I'm wondering how long I was out?

"Yes Jordan, I also paid for them. I knew we had to leave tomorrow so I got us the tickets. I hope you're not mad."

"Why would I be mad? You kept this journey for the treasure on track while I was, let's just say, napping? Remind me to pay you back when we get back from this journey." I smiled at her in gratitude for taking the initiative while I was out.

"Jordan, and Lilly I want you to have this, it once belonged to my Dad, but sadly he passed away, and I have no use for it now." Huko hands me what seems to some sort of musical instrument.

I shake my head trying to clear it. Things seem to be moving pretty quickly right now. "Huko, what is this?"

"Jordan, this is the flute of wolves. When you're in trouble, just let your instinct as a Prince of the Frost Wolf Tribe kick in. Play what you feel in your heart, and a pack of wolves will rush to your aide."

I take the flute, put it into my backpack, and thank Huko for the final gift. "Well Huko, Lilly and I should really be going."

"Jordan, I have one final gift for you." I laugh on the inside, and think how many gifts is this guy going to give me? "Jordan, this is the amulet of the first King of the Frost Wolf Tribe. He hand-crafted this amulet. It has been passed down for generations. I want you to keep this, and wear it." Huko places the amulet into my hand, and smiles at me. I open my mouth to thank him but he vanishes into thin air, along with the other Frost Wolf Tribe folk. I look around, thinking holy crap, what just happened?

I turn to look at Lilly with confusion and amazement. "This was only the first relic, and I just about lost my mind trying to wrap my head around this stuff. I do not blame you if you want to go back to Boston."

"I can't let you do this alone." Lilly grabs my hand, and squeezes it, "I mean after all you are the future King of the Frost Wolf Tribe. How can I abandon my King?" Lilly breaks out into laughter, and giggles, mock bowing down to me.

I crack up laughing as well. "Hey now, watch your tone around the future King of the Frost Wolf Tribe." Lilly continues to laugh. We head out to our car. "So, what did you think about that whole experience?"

"We could be back at Boston sitting in class right now, but instead we just found the Frost Wolf Tribe. I'm glad I came on this journey with you. Some experiences can't be learned in a classroom.

"We still have four more relics to get before we go to the Keeper of the Treasure. We best get driving to Colorado to catch tomorrow's flight." I start the car, and drive towards Colorado wondering what excitement Egypt holds for us.

Chapter 8: Egypt

I wake up to the alarm on my phone buzzing, and turn it off, rolling on to my side. I look over at Lilly who clearly got up before me.

"Well look who finally got up."

"Lilly, are you still sure you don't want to go back to Boston?"

"Yes, I'm sure. Now get yourself ready, we have a flight to catch!"

I clean up, and get ready. Flipping on the TV quick to see the score of the games from last night, the first channel programmed to come on is a news channel. *"If you are just joining us now, there is no update to the two University of Boston students who have been missing from college for days. The father of one of them is the famous Professor from Michigan University who currently holds the record for the*

Nobel Peace Prize. The search for the two students has had few leads and some are wondering how long the search will continue. The hope is that the two students will show up in Boston soon. If you have any information, please contact the number at the bottom of the screen. That's all from us here at Denver News Six, enjoy your morning."

"Lilly, do you realize what this means, they have no idea where we are. This is perfect!" I look at my phone, 7:00 am. "We need to get going." I sling my backpack over my shoulder, and head out towards the parking lot, Lilly, following close behind. We get in the car, and head towards the Denver International Airport. An hour later we get to the airport, and drop the car off at the car rental company. All the times I have been inside Denver International Airport it never gets old. The vibrant scenes, and the feeling of Colorado vibes are amazing. Colorado has always been one of my favorite states. We go through security, and heading towards the gate, by grumbling stomach reminds me I missed breakfast. "Lilly, I need to get some food." Walking towards a coffee shop, I order a coffee, an egg, and bagel sandwich, checking with Lilly to see if she wants to order anything.

"Your total is ten fifty." I reach for my card to pay but realize that I should pay with cash, or they might be able to track my spending purchases, to find me. The news bulletin is a wake-up call to be more careful from now on. I hand the clerk the money, and walk over towards Lilly who is sitting next to a young lady with her dog. I sit down next to Lilly, and the lady she is talking to stops to look at me.

"This must be your fiancé you were telling me about." I freeze, and wonder what she told this lady, but am glad it's not the truth, how we are two students from Boston University that cops are looking for. The lady offers me a hand shake, and I play along. "So, where are you two off to?"

"Egypt, we respond at the same time."

"Oh how quaint, off to see the pyramids?"

"Yes we are" I respond.

"Well you two love birds enjoy. I need to go board my flight to Scotland. I go every year to visit family in Inverness." The lady gets up and walks away.

I glare at Lilly, "Really, that's what you came up with?"

"The fiancé lie is always a strong lie. I wasn't going to tell her what is really going on in our lives."

"Well I guess you're right, but next time tell people we are just two friends on vacation." Lilly, nods in agreement, and we wait for our boarding.

The man at the counter for our flight gets on the speaker system, "Now boarding group A flight to Cairo Egypt.

"That's us," Lilly, says as she stands.

"I swear to god, if you booked first class seats...." I left the empty threat hanging. The agent scans our tickets, and we sit down in our seats, of course in first class. After we got settled in a flight attendant walks up to us.

"Hello, my name's Tina, and I will be serving you in the first class section. You have free Wi-Fi available, and the movie choices are listed on this card. We will be serving dinner tonight, and breakfast in the morning. Here are the menus if you'd like to select your meal choices. I'll be bringing warm cloths to wash with and your drink choices, including complimentary champagne as soon as the captain gives us clearance. If there is anything you need, please let me know.

"Thank you Tina, I'm good for now." Lilly does not respond. The flight attendant walks on to another first class passenger. I glance over to see what she's doing. Lilly has her laptop out, looking at something on her screen. "What are you doing," I ask curiously.

"While you were having a chat with Tina, I booked us a hotel for two nights in Cairo, got us a car, and found the map for where we need to go to get, the-you-know-what." She looks at me raising her eyebrows up and down, smiling.

"Wow! You did all that in like forty seconds. Maybe you should become a travel agent." Lilly laughs, and goes back to her laptop. She fires up a movie streaming platform, and begins to watch some love story movie. I pull out my phone, and look at it for the first time in a while. To my surprise, no texts or calls from Dad. I close my phone, and doze off.

We land in Cairo the following day. After the long flight we decide to find a café. Shortly after sitting down a man walks up to us and begins to speak to us in Arabic, the language in Egypt. He asks us what he can get us.

Lilly looks puzzled, "What did he say?"

"He said hello, and what can he get for us."

"You know Arabic?"

"I know over twenty five languages. When your Dad is a history professor you get a lot of languages taught to you. Many languages have slightly different dialects from surrounding regions." I respond to the man in Arabic, he nods, and thanks me.

She studies me for a moment, and then asks, "Are you still planning on leaving school after this?"

"Yes, I am."

"What about college?"

"I think I might go live with the Frost Wolf Tribe for a while. I'd like to study them some more, and maybe open a museum dedicated to the tribe. What about you? What's your plan after all this?

The server comes, and brings us our food, and Lilly's face turns blank, "Jordan what is this?"

"It's Bamia. It's a sweet and sour okra, it's good, try it."

Lilly is hesitant to try the food, but takes a bite, "Jordan this is amazing!" I turn to the server and tell him in Arabic that she likes the food, he smiles and bows in. As Lilly continues to eat I ask her again, "What do you plan to do after this?"

She stops eating and looks at me. "I was going to go back to college, but I want to keep spending time with you. Since you aren't going back, maybe I'll spend more time with you before I go back to college."

"Go to college. Don't worry about me, or what I am doing. You have to do what's best for you, and that's going to college, trust me. I can always come visit you anytime. Believe me though then I say, you should finish college." Lilly has small tears swelling in her eyes, but doesn't want to admit what I think she is feeling.

We finish the food, thank the server, and chefs, and head towards the hotel down the street. Looking around I see the city is bustling with scooters, cars, and tons of street vendors selling a variety of items. We walk into the hotel, and approach the front desk. The man behind the counter smiles, and greets us with a warm welcome, and gives us our room key. The room key says five- ten. We get in the elevator, and take it up to fifth floor, easily finding our room. My jaw drops in amazement of the room. The design of it is something I haven't seen before, and the view from the window shows pyramids in the background. I turn around to see Lilly has crawled into the bed and is already sleeping. I crawl into my bed, and begin to fade into a deep sleep.

I wake up the next morning, and get ready to head to the Temple of Osiris. We head to the main floor, locate our rental car, and head out towards the Temple. "So Jordan, is there going be people at this temple?"

"No, there shouldn't be anyone there. There was recently an earthquake near the Temple, so no one is going near it for a while." We get into the car, and drive towards the Temple. Lilly, passes the time by counting every pyramid she sees, but she stops to ask me questions.

"Jordan, do you think that we could maybe take a small break after this relic? I am starting to get a little exhausted."

"I'll tell you what, we will go to Scotland next, and you can hang out in the hotel, and sleep while I go get the relic. How does that sound?"

"I don't want you to have to go after a relic by yourself though."

"Don't worry about me. I'll be fine. You have to trust me when I say I will be fine."

"Are you sure you'll be fine?"

"Yes, I'm positive I can handle Scotland by myself." We continue to drive toward the Temple of Osiris, and in a matter of minutes the temple comes into view. I speed up to the temple, and park outside the entrance. "This is it, the Temple of Osiris. I personally believe it to be the best place in all of Egypt."

Lilly surveys the temple, "Where are we going inside this temple?"

"Well, the relic appears to be in an area of the temple that is a room dedicated to Anubis, the god of the dead." We walk towards the temple area, and enter the room dedicated to Anubis. As we walk into the room a vibe of mystery shrouds the place.

"So Jordan, where is it?"

I glance around the room, and see Anubis's staff on the altar of death. Approaching the altar, I run my hands along the staff. "Lilly, do you know the symbolism behind Anubis's staff?"

"I can't say that I do."

"This staff was responsible for transferring the emperor's from their burial tombs into after life." This staff could take a soul, and the body of a human when dead, and bring it into the Egyptian afterlife. Eventually Anubis got out of control, and began to kill innocent civilians in order to fulfill his lust for death. He was eventually killed, and his staff remained locked up for a long time." I pick up the staff, and suddenly a light shines through the room, and the staff begins to glow.

"Jordan, what's going on!"

I attempt to remain calm. I take the staff, and point it into the light coming into the room. Suddenly the light explodes, and glass shatters. Standing in front of us is Anubis. Lilly's jaw drops. Did we just summon the Egyptian god of death?

Anubis begins to speak. "Greetings those who have summoned me. I am the great Anubis, god of death. You are here for the relic of Egypt for the Copper Scroll treasure."

"Yes, great Anubis. I am Jordan and this is Lilly. We already have one of the five relics, and came to seek you out."

"Well Jordan, there is one way of testing if you got the first relic." With a snap of his fingers Anubis summons vipers into the room. Lilly shrieks, and jumps back, I instinctively take out the flute of wolves, and put my lips up to it. I begin to play a song I have never heard before, but like Huko said it would come naturally to me. Suddenly out of nowhere a pack of wolves comes charging into the room, and stand by my side waiting to strike. Anubis snaps his fingers, and the vipers disappear. I call the wolves off, and they run out of the room.

"Well Jordan, I am impressed you made it this far without freezing to death in that pond inside the cave to get the vase."

"Trust me Anubis, that wasn't a fun time."

"Jordan I can't just let you walk outside of this place with the relic without a test, you know that, right?"

"Yes Anubis, I understand. So what is this test you have for me?"

"I am going to have you jump off the top of this temple, and if you live, you get the relic."

My head says, are you kidding me?! My mouth says, "You got a deal Anubis." We walk outside to the temple grounds, and Lilly looks at me like I've completely lost my mind.

"Jordan, really? You can't live a twenty story fall. You are a mad man. Please don't do this. There has to be another way!"

I put my hand on Lilly's shoulder, "Lilly trust me, I can do this. I will live, I promise. Have I steered you wrong yet?"

Anubis points towards a ladder, "Here we are, the highest place in the temple. Twenty stories. I hope you are ready." I climb up the ladder, and get to the top. Once there I look down at Lilly and Anubis. Twenty stories is really high up. "Whenever you are ready Jordan." I run towards the edge, take a deep breath, and dive off, quickly falling down towards the sand below. Mid-way in the air I frantically rub the amulet Huko gave me, and instantly I am inside an ice crystal that lands on the ground breaking my fall. I dust my shoulders off and walk over to Anubis.

"Anubis, you know never to test a Frost Wolf Tribe Prince."

"Well done Jordan, you passed the test, and you convinced Huko to give you the amulet. You are the clearly the one to complete the journey."

"Alright Anubis, I proved myself, where is the relic at?" "

"What is earned is yours." I reach my hand out, and Anubis places a bag full of dust in my hand.

"What is this? This isn't the relic."

"No Jordan, it's not. Did you really think it would be that easy? You basically got the first relic handed to you, but in my domain you are not given the relic so easily!"

"What is it I have to do to get this relic?"

"I have one final test for you Jordan, and then you shall receive the relic of Egypt. In order to get the relic from me you must translate this ancient Egyptian wall art, and tell me word for word what it means."

"He can't do that!" Lilly, screams at Anubis, and he begins to laugh, but I press forward to the wall and look up at Anubis.

"Go on Jordan, tell me what these symbols are."

"Ok that's a Djed. That one is an Ankh. This one is a Tjet, and finally this one is an Udjat Eye."

"Impressive Jordan, you have defied death, summoned the wolves, and can identify ancient Egyptian symbols. You have passed all three of my tests."

"Great Anubis, now can I have the relic?"

"Not just quite yet."

"What do you mean not quite yet!? I did all three tests, give me the damn relic!"

"Sorry Jordan, I would love to give you the relic, but the last thing you need to do before I give you the relic is to talk to King Tut. He must ask you a few questions, then you can get your relic." Anubis begins to chant something and a portal opens up. King Tut walks out in a robe, and sits down on a chair. I can't believe my eyes that King Tut is here in front of me!

"Jordan is it?"

"Yes King Tut, sir."

"I am going to ask you a few questions if you don't mind. Jordan what is your main goal of this journey you are on?"

"Well King Tut, I want to find all the relics, claim the treasure from the Treasure Keeper, and bring all the relics, the Copper Scroll, and the treasure to the Qumran Library where it belongs sir."

King Tut nods his head. "OK Jordan, next question. Will you Jordan do everything humanly possible to get your journey completed, even if it means risking your own life?"

"Yes King Tut, I would risk my life to complete this journey."

King Tut nods his head. "OK Jordan, last question. Will you keep everything that occurs on this journey secret, and tell people a less complex version of how you found the treasure?"

"Yes King Tut, I will."

King Tut nods, smiles, and stands up. "Anubis, please give him the relic. He is worthy of being the one to collect all five relics, and be the first to find the treasure." I hold my hand out, and Anubis places the relic into my hand. I look down, and see an Ankh.

"Jordan, I present to you the Ankh of Anubis, the second relic of the five. With this relic comes great responsibility. It is only to touch the hands of the Treasure Keeper. Now run along to Scotland, and complete your legacy Jordan." Suddenly Anubis, and King Tut vanish into thin air.

I look over at Lilly to see how she is handling all of this. She's standing there with no emotion on her face. "Lilly, you just saw King Tut, and Anubis. You're not even surprised by this?"

"Well Jordan, I mean we already met the Frost Wolf Tribe, and now this. I guess I'm getting used to crazy stuff during this journey."

"I don't want you to feel like you aren't doing anything to help. You have done so much for me already."

"Jordan this is your legacy to complete. This is your show, you are the main event. I excited and happy that you asked me to come along and share this journey with you." We hop into the car, and drive back towards Cairo, and Lilly begins to laugh out of the blue. "This journey has been insane, but like I said, when we get to Scotland I need a day to rest in the hotel room."

I nod my head, and continue to drive the car back to Cairo. Abruptly I pull over and stop the car. Turning to Lilly I say, "I want a straight honest answer out of you, no beating around the bush, got it?"

"Yes. I understand."

"Lilly, do you have feelings for me, because I keep getting this vibe from you whenever it's just the two of us around that you are giving off signs."

"I don't follow," she responds.

"Well, like for example, at the cafe yesterday, you were starting to tear up when I said I wouldn't be going back to Boston after this is all over."

"I do have feelings for you, but I have to put them aside during this journey. I am here to help you find the relics, and the treasure. That's all."

Disappointed, I pull back out onto the road and continue to drive back to Cairo. We eventually arrive into downtown Cairo, and park the car. Heading into the hotel for our last night in Egypt I think about tomorrow as we are heading to Inverness. We're both exhausted and I soon climb into bed. Out of the corner of my eye, right before I fall asleep, I think I see Lilly in her bed quietly sobbing, but it's too late for me as my eyes are closing, and I hit a deep sleep.

I wake up in the morning to the smell of coffee brewing from the cafe across the street. Lilly, is already packed, and ready to go. "Lilly, are you ready to go to Scotland? Our flight is in two hours."

"Yes, I'm ready."

"Look, I know you have to put your feelings on hold, and we are probably going in different directions when this is all over. I'll make you a promise. If at all possible, I will visit you every other week in Boston."

"You don't have to do that you know."

"Trust me, I want to, but right now my focus is on the remaining three relics. We smile at each other in understanding. "What do you say we head to Inverness, and you can rest in town while I go out, and find the relic?" She nods and finished putting together the last of her gear. I pack my stuff up, and we head off to the Cairo airport. Lilly runs over to a coffee shop getting a much needed coffee, and I take out my phone, turning the camera onto myself. I look different from when we left. In a few weeks my hair got longer, my facial hair is longer, and my face looks different, more aged maybe? I almost don't recognize who I am anymore.

Lilly comes back with her coffee, sits down, and begins to sip her coffee. The desk agent begins to call the boarding groups. We get up, board the plane, and sit in our seats. The flight takes off, and for most of the flight Lilly is fast asleep. I pull my phone out, and scroll through photos. I stumble upon one of my Dad at the grand opening of his museum that he opened in Dallas. The other photos I scroll through bring up so many memories. I know that he is probably freaking out that I am probably dead, and the heaviness of my guilt weighs on me that I'm putting him through that. I wake Lilly up from her slumber as we are landing, and we debark from the plane. Walking through the Inverness airport, we notice the extreme change of scenery from Egypt. Seeing grass outside was a nice change after spending the previous days in the desert. We leave the airport, pick up our rental car, and begin to drive to the hotel. Checking into our room I sort through my gear bringing only what I think I'll need.

Lilly looks over at me unsure, "Are you positive you will be fine without me?"

I smile at her, "Yes, I'll be fine, just have fun, and get some rest." With that I walk out the door.

Chapter 9: Scotland Relic

Back in the rental car, I make my way towards the Northern Highlands where the relic is rumored to be. I drive for what seems to be hours. Without Lilly's constant chatter I scan through radio stations. Although Scottish music is a nice change from music in the United States, I eventually find myself tired of listening to the radio. One thing about driving alone in silence is you get time to think about things. I feel bad for leaving Lilly and doing this without her. Part of me wishes she were here enjoying this next adventure with me, especially after all she's done for me. But then I remember her telling me she really wanted some down time to rest. I resolve that this relic hunt will be mine journey alone.

Finally arriving at the Northern Highlands, I pull my notes out on the Scotland relic. It appears to be simple enough. I just have to go to this spot on the map, simple enough. As I begin to walk I suddenly feel a presence behind me. Turning around quickly, I call out, "Can I help you?" There in front of me is an old man with long white hair, a big beard, blue robes, and a staff.

"Hello Jordan, you are ahead of schedule. I had to hurry to get here."

"Merlin?"

"Well this sure ain't your grandpa is it?" Anubis told me there was someone traveling with you, where is that person?"

"She is back in Inverness resting." I'm trying to catch my mind up with the fact that I'm standing here chatting with Merlin.

"Well Jordan, I hope you are ready for the test I have for you."

"I am ready Merlin, let's get this done."

"Excellent I assume you have the Ankh from the Temple of Osiris with you."

"Got it right here." I pull the Ankh out of my backpack, look at it, and flip it over.

"Now that you have the Ankh, you should be able to do this no problem. Do you see this animal that has recently passed away of old age? The test is to see if you can bring it back to life, thus letting its life cycle reset."

I take the Ankh, point it at the animal, and a blue beam emits from the Ankh. The animal begins to breathe."

"You did it Jordan! The animal will get to experience a full life again thanks to you. I have one more test for you before I can give you the relic of Scotland." I'm thinking, there always seems to be just one more test. Merlin takes his staff, bangs it into the ground five times, and suddenly an arena rises up from the ground. The grass turns to dirt, dust, and a full blood sport arena takes shape around us. Merlin takes his staff, pointing it to the sky. A dragon flies in from the distance, and lands inside the arena, spitting out a breath of fire. Out of nowhere the stands are full of people from a time period long ago. I'm thinking, this is not looking good for me.

"Ladies and gentlemen welcome to the event of a lifetime. In the right corner of the arena is the current living human who is chasing the third relic for the Copper Scroll treasure. To the left is a fierce dragon. The two will fight to the death. If this human, Jordan, claims victory, he will be awarded the third relic." I take a deep breath and swallow the lump in the back of my throat. What have I gotten into now?

Merlin bangs his staff into the ground one last time, and a variety of pillars sprout from the ground. Attached to them is a rack of medieval weapons.

"Chose any weapon of choice." I walk over to the weapon rack, and take a sword, thinking, only one? Somehow this doesn't seem fair. Merlin screams out, "Let the battle begin!"

The dragon rises up and flies around the arena spewing fireballs at me. I have no game plane other than to keep dodging his fireballs. Think! A plan of attack would be really good right about now. I pull out the amulet of wolves, rub it, and a large wolf comes bursting into the arena, standing next to me. I climb onto the seven foot tall wolf, and begin weaving in and out of pillars. "Listen up wolf, on my cue I want you to run up that pillar in the far left corner!" I continue to weave in and out of pillars, dodging fireballs. I whistle, and the wolf runs up the pillar. As we reach the top I leap off the wolf, who then runs down to the arena floor. The dragon begins to fly towards me. I take out my flute that Huko gave me, and let my instinct take over. I play the song with haste as the dragon is nearly on top of me, and as I hit the last note, an ice beam bursts out of the flute, hitting the dragon in the chest. It falls to the arena floor.

The crowd bursts into cheers. Merlin silences the crowd with his hand. "Ladies and Gentlemen, the dragon is slain! I present to Jordan, the relic of Scotland!" Merlin hands me the relic of Scotland.

"Merlin, what is this?"

"That Jordan is the sword that belonged to King Arthur, please use it wisely." I'm thinking, Holy Shit, King Arthur's sword? "Where are you off to next Jordan?"

A little out of breath and overwhelmed with this relic, I respond, "Well, all that's left is Japan and Australia. I need to get back to Lilly though, she's waiting for me back in Inverness." Merlin takes his staff, and holding it out, points it at me. Within a second I find myself in an alley in Inverness. Wow, that sure beats walking. Wonder what the rental car company will say about the car I left there?

I head to the hotel to meet Lilly, and as I open the hotel room I find it's empty. I search for Lilly, finding only a note on the bed. *"Dear Jordan, I went out to look for you. I rented a car, and am heading towards the Northern Highlands right now."* In the bottom left corner is noted the time she left, noon. Great so Lilly is out walking towards the Northern Highlands, and I am not even there anymore. I review my options. Racing out of the hotel, I notice how dark it's gotten. I dodge into the closest back road, and furiously rub the amulet. Within seconds a large wolf appears in front of me. I leap onto the wolf, and instruct us to follow the path of Lilly to find her. I only hope she hasn't run into any trouble. Thankfully the full moon lights our way.

Instead of following the main road, the wolf takes me deep into a forest outside of town and nudges me off its back. I stare into the wolf's eyes, and through some sort of telepathy, I hear the wolf telling me to use the sword from King Arthur. I pull the sword out, and jam it into the ground. Suddenly the ground begins to shake. Holding onto the hilt, I quickly pull the sword back out of the ground. Nothing happens. Great, I have a defective sword. Then, off in the distance I hear the sound of rushing water. It gets louder as if the water is flooding towards me. I frantically look around for something to stand on to avoid getting washed away. Within seconds, a woman riding a current of water, stops in front of me. The water stops flowing as well. It all just stops right in front of me. OK, I'm thinking, crazy weird.

"You have summoned the lady of the lake, what it is you need."

"I need to get to the Northern Highlands right away!"

With a snap of a finger the lady of the lake creates a circle in the water, "Jump into the water child, and you will be there in a moment's notice." I plunge into the water, and begin to spin around as if in a vortex. Suddenly, I rise up from the lake finding myself near the Northern Highlands. I can see Lilly looking around in the distance for me. I begin to swim to her, and as I struggle to get to land Lilly vanishes out of sight.

I finally reach land, and am confused as to where she might have gone. I play the flute Huko gave me, and three wolves come leaping towards me, halting at my side. "Wolves, Lilly is currently lost in the Highlands. I need you to spread out, and find her.

Bring her to me, I will stay right here. The wolves fan out into different directions, and I wait for their return. My mind plays several scenarios as to what could have happened to her, none of them are good. One wolf comes back, and reports seeing nothing. The second wolf soon returns as well with the same report. I begin to panic.

After an hour, the third wolf comes sprinting towards me with Lilly on its back. Using the strange telepathic communication we have it communicates, "Prince Jordan sir, Lilly is hurt. She needs medical attention quickly."

"Thank you for finding her. You two wolves can leave, I will only need this one to further assist me." The third wolf shapeshifts into a half human-half wolf form, and we begin to look at her wounds.

The wolf tells me, "Prince Jordan, it appears she has a gash on her left arm, and a swollen foot what do you advise we do sir?"

"I have an idea. It's a little out there, but it might just work." I take the Ankh from Osiris Temple, and aim it at Lilly's gashed arm. A yellow beam comes out of the Ankh, and Lilly's gash disappears. I take the Ankh, and aim it at her foot, another yellow beam shoots from the Ankh and also disappears.

"Sir she is still unconscious, and not responding."

"We just have to wait for her to wake up. Can you take her to the hospital in Inverness?" Without hesitation the half wolf-half man transforms back into a wolf. I put Lilly onto his harness, and he rides off into the night. Well great, now how do I get back to Inverness? I take the sword out, and am about to jam it into the ground, but a flashing light blinds my eyes.

"Merlin why are you here?"

"Try to limit the uses on the sword Jordan.
Here take this portal. Use it and you'll find yourself in
the alley right behind Inverness Hospital." Merlin
creates a glowing blue portal, and I hop into it. I step
out into the alley, and dust myself off. Walking quickly
into the hospital, I head to the front desk.

"Hello, I am looking for my friend Lilly. I think
she just arrived here."

"Lilly, Lilly, ah yes we have a Lilly in room
142." I sprint down the hall, and into the hospital
room to find Lilly in a bed. I walk up to the bed, and
look down at her. She looks lifeless. "

Excuse me, who might you be?" I turn around
to see a doctor standing in the doorway.

"I am her friend Jordan. Is she going to be
alright?"

"She just suffered a knock to the head it appears. She should be up, and moving around by tomorrow morning. We want to keep her overnight for observation."

"Can I stay here with her tonight doctor?"

"I don't see why not." The doctor leaves the room, and I sit in a chair on the far side of the room. I'm so thankful she's ok. As I sit there, the exhaustion of the day catches up to me, and I fall asleep.

I wake up the next morning to see Lilly awake, and talking to the nurse. "Well hello sleepy head, looks like you finally woke up." I run over to Lilly, and grasp her hand.

"I will leave you two alone," the nurse says, leaving the room, and closing the door behind her.

"Jordan, how is my gash, and foot swelling gone already?"

"Don't worry about it Lilly, what matters is you are alright."

"I should have stayed at the hotel, and waited for you. I'm sorry."

"No it's my fault."

"Well Jordan do you have it?" I pull out the sword, and show it to Lilly.

"Wow! What did you have to do to get it?"

I talked to her for about an hour leaving out no details of the entire fight with the dragon, Merlin, finding her note, the power of the sword, and how she got to the hospital.

"That sounds like one crazy day. If I hadn't already experienced your crazy journey, I probably wouldn't believe this story."

"Our flight to Australia is in six hours, are you well enough to come with me?"

"Trust me Jordan, I am fine. I wouldn't dare let you go without me."

I leave her to go and get the doctor to check her out of the hospital. We have a flight to catch, and a relic to find.

Chapter 10: Australian Relic

As Lilly and I leave the hospital we see a car parked out front with an envelope on the windshield, addressed to me. *"Dear Jordan, the wolves informed me of everything. I called a car company in Inverness and asked them to deliver a car to the hospital for you so you won't miss your flight."* The note was from Huko. Wow, I'm over-whelmed with gratitude. We get into the car, and drive off to the airport. Dropping the car off at the car rental counter, we walk to our gate for the flight to Australia. Eventually the boarding begins, and we take our seats. I look out the window as the plane lifts off, and briefly reminisce all of the incredible events we experienced in Inverness. Turning my attention to my laptop, I browse the news. After stopping in Moscow for a pit stop we resume the flight, and land in Melbourne a few hours later.

We debark the plane and walk out into the bright atmosphere of Melbourne, instantly feeling the warmth. After getting our rental car we drive to the hotel, check in to our room, toss our stuff in the room, and Lilly immediately crawls into bed. We are both exhausted from the lengthy trip.

As we are stretching out in bed I tell her about this relic. "There is a place called Uluru. It's a sacred rock formation basically in the middle of nowhere, and apparently the relic is inside the rock formation."

"Jordan how are you going to get inside Uluru, it's a giant rock."

"With this!" I pull out the sword, and run my hand along the blade. This blade will shatter the rocks opening, and expose the entrance for me. Are you coming with me on this one?" Lilly waits for a while to respond, and I actually think she may have fallen asleep. Looking over I notice she is nodding her head. "Alright then, we can catch about four hours of sleep and then we need to hit the road. It's a ten hour car ride to Uluru." Lilly groans, rolls over and is asleep almost immediately. I set the alarm and pass out myself.

I wake up all too soon to the sound of my alarm. We crawl out of the bed and pack up the car, driving off into the morning sun. Lilly is amazed by all the wildlife that is packed into Australia, and can't stop taking photos of them. We talk about our favorite memories growing up. Lilly tells me about the time she got to meet a famous singer. We keep driving for what seems like forever, and finally stop to take a break, eat some food, and get back on the road. Uluru finally comes into view, and the rock formation is even more wonderful than I imagine. I am filled with wonder as we drive towards it. "Well Lilly we are here."

"So what now?"

"It says, find the symbol of the snake, and let the power of the sword show you the way." We walk along Uluru for a while, and eventually stumble upon the snake symbol. Taking the sword of King Arthur, I jam it into the rock. The rock formation begins to shake, and a square slot opens up from the rock formation. Looking at each other, we walk into the dark passage. I grab the torch sitting on a wall, and scan the room. Lilly shrieks and grabs on to me. The room is filled with statues of animals, mainly of snakes. But that's not why she shrieked, an actual snake was slithering towards us, and it wasn't small. I draw the sword, ready to strike, but the snake shapeshifts into a human.

"Hello humans. I am King Viprus, the Snake King of Australia. I assume you two are here for the fourth relic."

"Yes King Viprus, we already have the relics from America, Scotland, and Egypt. All that's left is Australia, and Japan."

"Well you are so close to completing the journey, and for that I must applaud you on making it this far."

"So King Viprus, what is the test you have for me?"

"There are three tests you must pass in order to get the relic of Australia from me." I'm thinking, well at least this guy is honest right from the start. Not one, and then another, and another. He just comes right out and says, three! He continues, "The first thing you must do is speak to a snake. The second, you must bring water to these caves so the animals have fresh water to drink. Lastly, you must find your way back out of Uluru. Shall we begin Jordan?"

These don't sound too terrible. "I am ready King Viprus." Viprus summons a snake. I take out the flute of wolves, and I transform into a wolf. I begin to speak to the snake, and the snake responds along with a few hisses. After a few more seconds the snake slithers off into the cave, out of sight. I transform back into a human, and King Viprus bows in acknowledgment of my success.

"Alright Jordan, next you must provide this cave with water." I take the sword out, and thrust it into the ground. The Lady of the Lake appears.

"Jordan, what do you require from me?"

"Lady of the Lake, I require this cave to flow with water!" She snaps her finger, and a bubble of water drops from the top of the cave bursting into every direction possible. The water begins to fill in the dried ground. King Viprus again bows in acknowledgment of my success.

"Alright Jordan, the last thing you must do is escape the Uluru, and I will give you the relic!" Viprus vanishes, and we begin to walk through the cave, but alas we keep getting lost around every turn.

"Jordan, how do we get out of here?" Lilly is beginning to sound worried. I think of the options, and pull out the flute of wolves. I begin to play a song, and suddenly a wolf comes running towards us.

"Prince Jordan, I am at your service sir!"

"Wolf, I need you to help us find a way out of this cave."

"Not a problem Prince Jordan, you can count on me!" The wolf sprints off into the distance, and Lilly and I continue to explore the cave.

She stops to stare and something and asks, "Jordan what's this thing?" I come over, and take a look at the odd figurine of a snake.

"This is it! This is our way out!" I take the figurine, and put it on the ground, and crush it with the sword.

"Jordan what you doing!"

"Trust me on this Lilly." The figurine emits a green essence, and suddenly we are both transformed into snakes.

"Damnit Jordan, see what you did now!"

"Trust me Lilly, this is what we need to do, follow me." We begin to slither around the cave until we get up to a pipe. "See, we need to go through here, and we come out on the outside." We slither through the pipe, plop out of the pipe, and waiting for us is King Viprus.

"Well done you two, now I will transform you back into humans." He snaps his finger, and we return to our human bodies. "Jordan, how did you know to break the figurine with the sword of King Arthur?"

I reply, "There is an old saying about the sword and the snake."

"Well Jordan this is the fourth relic. It's hard to believe you are almost done with this journey."

"So what's this relics powers," I ask King Viprus.

"Well with this relic you can transform into a snake, but keep in mind if you play the flute, and transform into a wolf you must go back to your human state if you wish to use the relic. I look at the relic and it's a snake ring.

"So Lilly, are you ready for the last relic?"

She gladly responds, "Yes! We should head back to Melbourne." We say goodbye to King Viprus, and we head back to Melbourne.

"Jordan, where did you hear that saying from?"

"What saying, the one about the sword, and the snake?"

"Yes that one." "

My mom always told me a bedtime story about the snake, and the sword. It's a classic fable in our house." We drive for hours, and finally pull up to the hotel. Getting into our room, we crash on the bed hard.

I wake up in the morning, and Lilly is already packed and ready to go to Japan. "Well good morning sleepy head, are you ready to go complete your legacy today?" I smile, and nod at Lilly. We gather up our stuff and head over to the Melbourne airport. We head through security, and get to our gate. Lilly spends her time looking at hats at a local shop while I try to collect my thoughts about what today will be like. We board the plane, and begin our flight to Japan.

Chapter 11: Japan Relic

We arrive in Japan, and head out to get our car. It seems like we've been doing that a lot lately. As we drive to a cafe for some food I begin to explain to Lilly all about this relic, and where it's located at The Island Shrine of Itsukushima. After stopping at the café to relax a bit and have a meal we drive to the Island Shrine. Lilly talks to me the entire ride about how she thinks her favorite period of time is ancient Greece. We drive past lush trees, and Lilly points out monkeys on the side of the road.

We finally arrive at the Island Shrine. In the water stands the shrine. Nothing happens for a while, and then all of a sudden the water sprays up into the air spewing water everywhere. A figure comes flying out of the water and up onto land.

"Hello Jordan, I am Tokugawa Ieyasu, and you are here for the final relic."

"Tokugawa Ieyasu, it's an honor sir." I kneel down, and Lilly follows my lead. "Lilly, this is Tokugawa Ieyasu, the founder of the first Shogun, and my favorite historical person from Asia. So Tokugawa, this final relic is where?"

"Well Jordan, you must pass the test of the Shogun in order to get this relic."

"So what is this Shogun test?"

"You will be taken back in time to when Japan is under siege from attack, and lead the Shogun into battle. Fail in the past, and you will not get the relic."

"Lilly I am doing this alone, I can't risk anything."

"Please let me help!"

"Sorry Lilly, my mind is made up."

Tokugawa summons a swirl in the water around the shrine, and suddenly in a matter of seconds I am transported to Japan, era 1570. "Left side men!" I hear screaming and shouting from Shogun men. "There you are general, what took you so long? What are the orders general?"

I look around, and survey the land, "Alright men, we move as one single unit to the left flank.

"What about the right flank general?"

"Leave that to me!" The Shogun fighters charge the left of the castle. I take a step back, pull out the flute, and begin to play. I keep playing, and take the snake ring, and put it inside the flute. In the distance hundreds of wolves come charging, followed by thousands of snakes slithering on the ground, except they aren't snakes but half snake- half human. The thousands of them stand at attention. "Snake men, wolf men the fate of the Copper Scroll Treasure is in our hands. Unite and defend the invasion!" The troops scream, and charge to the right side of the castle. I wait for hours when all the sudden I vanish, and appear back by the Island Shrine.

"Jordan are you alright?"

"Yes, I think I am."

Tokugawa asks me, "How did you know to insert the ring in the flute?"

"Well Tokugawa, I figured combining the power of turning into snake from the ring, combined with the flute song that summons wolves would summon half snake-half humans. So Tokugawa, where is this relic?"

"Right here Jordan." I put my hand out, and Tokugawa places the relic in my hand.

"What is this Tokugawa?"

"It's the Shogun Shrine Mirror, a very powerful disc." I take the disc, and examine it.

"So what does it do?"

"That Jordan, summons Shogun soldiers. Jordan, you need to prepare for the Treasure Keeper tomorrow."

"So where do I find this Treasure Keeper?"

"When you are ready, line your relics, and the Treasure Keeper will be summoned to come get you."

We drive the long journey back to our hotel for the night, and try to get some sleep. My mind whirls with all the possibilities of what I may be required to deal with tomorrow.

We wake up, and head out to Mt. Fuji to line up the relics. I take out the five relics, and line them up next to each other. The sun fades, and a blue moon rises up, giving an earie glow up us and the relics.

A sound rings out in the distance "The legacy of the treasure is almost complete! I will now bring you to the Treasure Keeper. Grab your relics, and stand ready." As I pick up the relics, Mt. Fuji begins to crumble. Snow falls down the mountain, rocks sliding, we prepare for the worst. A giant rush of snow comes pounding down the hill, and sweeps us away.

Chapter 12: The Legacy

"Jordan where are we?"

"I am not sure Lilly. That avalanche swept us away, and we ended up here."

A voice comes to us from a distance. "Jordan and Lilly, how nice of you to join me here. I assume you have the five relics?"

"Who are you?"

The man turns the corner, "I am the Treasure Keeper, and you two are the ones with the five relics."

"Where are we Treasure Keeper?"

"Isn't it obvious? You are in the ship that sunk carrying the Copper Scroll, what a most fitting place." I look around the Italian ship, and see pictures of Napoleon. "So how does it feel Jordan, to meet the Frost Wolf Tribe, Anubis, King Tut, Merlin, The Snake King, and Tokugawa?"

"Amazing sir, this whole journey was amazing!"

"So you will listen to me closely. You are to hand me the relics. I will give you the treasure. You will take the relics, treasure, and Copper Scroll to the library in Qumran. You will speak to the person in charge of the library. Say nothing other than that these belong here. Do you understand me?"

"Yes sir"

"After that you are going to never speak to anyone other than Lilly about this whole thing. This is a secret you take with you to the grave. Do you understand?"

"Yes sir!" The Treasure Keeper takes something from his pocket, and hands it to me.

"Sir what is this?"

"It's the treasure Jordan. Not all treasure is gold or silver."

"It's a map, and a compass?

"Yes Jordan, this is the map that will lead you to the Library of Alexandria, and this compass is the Compass of Napoleon."

"Napoleon knew where to find the library?"

"Yes Jordan. You are going to bring these to the Qumran Library. In five years you are going to take control of the Qumran Library as owner, and you are going to find the Library of Alexandria." I begin to open my mouth but the Treasure Keeper silences me. He snaps his finger, and suddenly we are a short walk from Qumran Library.

We begin to walk towards the library, and as we talk we reminisce of the journey we had. We walk up to the library door, and I knock on the door. A man opens the door.

"Yes, how can I help you two?"

"Sir, I think these belong to you, and the library." I hand him the bag with the Copper Scroll, the relics, the map, and compass.

His eyes open wide, "How did you get these?"

"Sorry sir, I am not allowed to say that."

"Well however you got these, I appreciate what you are doing for history, and this library." I begin to walk away, and the man yells out to me. "Sir who are you?"

I turn to look at him. "That's not important. What is important is that these are back in the Qumran Library. He nods his head, and walks back inside the library.

Lilly and I make our way back to Tel Aviv, and then book a flight to Boston. We sit on the plane, I look at Lilly as she sleeps hard. My mind whirls with all we've been through, and where we will be going next.

We land in Boston, and exit the airport area to get a taxi back to the college. The taxi driver looks at us, and smiles "Well look who is back in Boston!"

"I am sorry sir, do I know you?"

"I am the taxi driver who dropped you off at the airport when you left. People are going to be happy to see you." The taxi driver takes us to the campus, and asks us where we went. I smile at him and tell him we couldn't say. With that, we step out of the taxi and walk back onto the campus grounds.

Chapter 13: Life after a Legacy

Lilly and I look at each other and smile. We both feel the strangeness of being back at school. A student spots us, "Hey everyone, they are back!" A flock of students run toward us, asking us a million questions. I quickly silence them by telling them that we can't talk about anything we've just experienced. The crowd breaks up, and standing in the grass is professor Pelz.

"Well, if it isn't my favorite students."

"Hi professor Pelz," I mumble looking sheepishly at the ground.

"You know that you're going to need to spend a lot of time catching up."

"Sir, I won't be coming back to college. I am simply here to say goodbye to Lilly." He looks at me knowingly, nods, and leaves us to talk.

"Well Lilly, this is your stop, I don't want to keep you from your friends." Lilly walks up to me, and hugs me.

"Jordan, you promised you will come visit me," tears stand in her eyes.

"I will visit every weekend, you can count on it." Lilly stands firm as she watches me walk away. I also feel the sadness of our parting.

I locate my car, and begin the long drive to Ann Arbor to see my Dad. Putting in my favorite music, I settle in for the twenty hours it takes for me to get there. Arriving outside his office building, I take a deep breath and head in. I still have the keys he gave me years ago, and let myself into his office. It's early yet so I sit in his chair, kick back and catch a few winks while I wait for him to get to work.

I wake to find my dad staring down at me. I try to read his face so I would know how much trouble I was in "Hello Dad."

"Jordan what are you doing here?"

"I did it Dad, I can't say exactly what, but I think you know."

He shakes his head, "Jordan, there is no possible way."

My smile is huge, "Yes dad there is. Also, I am done at Boston, I have a promise to keep."

"I know you can't tell me everything, but you risked your life, I'm glad you did, and even more glad you are safely back home." He hugs me, and shakes my hand. "So, what do you say we go home, you take a shower, and then we go out to get something decent to eat."

I laugh out loud. "Sounds great Dad." We walk out of his office as he catches me up on what's been going on in the sports world. We get into his car, and drive towards the house.

"Jordan, just promise me, no more adventures like this."

I smile and wink at him, "Sorry Dad, like I said, I got a promise to keep."

"Just next time you leave for a while, at least let me know you are going off to do something crazy."

"You got it Dad"

"So what do you say before you leave to do whatever it is you have to do, you agree to be talk to the Dean about teaching a semester at the University of Michigan as a Teacher's Assistant.

"One semester only Dad." We drive into the night, and all I can think about is looking for the Library of Alexandria.

About The Author

Daniel Wiitanen is currently a college student pursuing his Masters in History. His plan after college is to become a Professor at a Junior University. His major influence in college came from his favorite History Professor Dr. Pelz, who sadly passed away in 2017. He was an inspiration to his students, and all those whom he took the time to share his love of history with.

www.ingramcontent.com/pod-product-compliance
Lightning Source LLC
Chambersburg PA
CBHW070923130626
46555CB00001B/255